Finding Keepers

Kristi Strong

Finding Keepers

ISBN: 069202249X
ISBN 13: 978-0692022498

Acknowledgments

~ This one is for Tyler. ~
I would have never survived high school without him.

To all the people who have made this possible, I can only offer my heartfelt gratitude a million times over.

To Sheila Bullock, my anchor as I plunged into the world of foster care. She helped me navigate the legal system to bring you an accurate story, and it broke my heart that for every event I thought up for Alyssa, she had helped a child get through worse. She is "Jessica," for so many students, their rock, their cheerleader, their kick-in-the-pants, and their guiding light.

To my parents, for giving me such a stable home that I can get lost in the dark worlds I create because I know that there is an open door at the end of the road, always.

To Kristina, for always forgiving my stupid grammar mistakes, and being an awesome enough friend to tell me when entire chapters need to be redone.

To the ladies of S4S, because where would I be without you guys? I know where I'd be, still stuck trying to figure out why I couldn't get *whatever* to work correctly.

And to every single person out there who has gone through a rough patch. I've read and heard so many stories, and your courage is amazing.

One

It towered over her, red bricks surrounded by white mortar, a wall stretching high above her head and blocking out the morning sunlight. A breeze ruffled the long, dark brown hair that had escaped the hood of her jacket, and she could hear clanking and rustling as the wind touched the flag pole beside her. A bell rang from inside the building, piercing the cold winter air, and the people around her scurried through the metal doors, checking the time on their cell phones as they went.

Another first day, she couldn't help but think with a resigned heaviness, praying that the bell she heard wasn't an indicator that she was late on her first day of school. This would mark Alyssa's tenth "first day" in the last six years, and it never got easier. Ever since her eyes opened one hour earlier, her stomach had been tied in knots at the thought of walking through a new set of doors, navigating a new maze of hallways, and feeling the curious and judging stares of her new peers.

A voice behind her caused Alyssa to turn, shifting her well-worn purple backpack onto her left shoulder.

While the backpack was old, the rest of her outfit was new, courtesy of her new foster parent, Jessica Sona. Alyssa used a gloved hand to pull a stray lock of hair from her eyes, both cautious and grateful that her newest keeper, her term for her foster guardians, was putting more effort into her first day at school than many others had done in the past.

"Try to have a good day, okay? I'll see you when you get home." Miss Sona had stepped out of the car and was leaning against the side. Alyssa felt a small pang of envy looking at her, impeccably dressed for her job at the town bank, the chocolate-brown suit looking natural on Miss Sona's slender body and her black hair styled in a sophisticated bob.

That morning had been their first time sharing the bathroom while each got dressed for the day, and Alyssa had been pleasantly surprised by how easy it had been. The night before, Miss Sona had asked when Alyssa wanted to start getting ready for the day, and had already showered before Alyssa was awake. By the time Alyssa needed to use the bathroom to get ready, a routine that rarely consisted of more than quickly washing her face, brushing her teeth, and staring dismally at her gaunt face and lack-luster hair, the bathroom was free for her use.

It was a far cry from her last home, where two teenaged girls and two adults shared one bathroom, and mornings were an exercise in organized chaos. Alyssa could only imagine how much worse it would have been if she actually cared about her appearance and needed a mirror to get ready for the day. She made sure that her time in the bathroom was five minutes or less, careful to never impose on anyone else's needs.

"I'll try, Miss Sona." Her lips turned up in a forced smile as she waved and took a deep breath of the biting air. Snow crunched under her new boots as she carefully hurried down the sidewalk and up the front steps. It was hard enough having to be the new girl at a high school, but being a new girl in January was a double challenge.

At least this school looks nicer than the last, Alyssa thought as she took in the large welcome mat at the front door, shining tile floors, and unmarred white walls. Students scurried through the hallway, rushing to their classes before the final bell rang, sending the last furtive text message, or desperately trying to finish their homework before the teacher noticed.

Standing in the middle of the intersection, staring at the starburst pattern of hallways in front of her, Alyssa immediately felt the butterflies in her stomach flap wildly as she realized how alone and overwhelmed she would be in this new school.

"You look lost," a pleasant but gravelly voice said from her right.

The polite smile plastered itself on her face at the sound. "Just getting my bearings," she replied, looking down at the pink sheet of paper that held her class schedule. *Would it kill them to provide a map with this?* She silently grumbled to herself as she tried to surreptitiously look at the numbers on the doors and figure out the system.

The owner of the voice pushed off the wall and stepped closer to her, his chain-link belt clinking as he leaned over her shoulder to look at the schedule. "Where's your first class? I can at least point you down the right path of the labyrinth."

A frustrated sigh almost escaped before she suppressed it. *Great, first day and already attracting the wrong attention.* It was not that she was anti-social, not exactly; she just had no time or energy to devote to developing relationships of any sort. Besides, friendships just made it harder when the white car pulled up and took her to a new town, new school, and new life.

She glanced over at him, not wanting to encourage his attention, but needing to scope him out. He was exactly the type that she needed to stay away from if she wanted to have some semblance of a stable life. Light brown hair had been morphed into a three-inch mohawk that ran along the top of his head, and he sported both a lip ring and a bar through his brow. A black leather jacket, black jeans, and silver-studded boots completed the ensemble. Alyssa could also see the worn crease of his pants pocket where a pack of cigarettes likely lived when he was out of school, and would bet money that tobacco was not the only thing he smoked.

I cannot associate myself with him, she thought harshly, *not if I want to make something out of my life.* Nice on the inside or not, she had to pay attention to the appearance of the crowd around her, because that was the crowd her new keeper would see, and that was what her judgment would be based upon.

His gray eyes flickered down and she realized he was still waiting for the answer. A blush crept up her cheeks as she responded, "um, English, in room four twenty-one." Her eyes glanced down the intersection again. *Why the heck don't schools have signs or something to go with the maps they should hand out*, she thought, embarrassed and angry that she had lasted less than five minutes before needing help.

The boy's lips twitched as he suppressed a grin. "I was just heading there myself. Come on, new girl, I'll show you where it is."

The words, "no thank you," froze on Alyssa's lips when she saw how his gray eyes softened at the look of equal measures panic and gratefulness she knew was on her face. Something in her relaxed at the blend of amusement and understanding, and it shook her to the core. She knew it was not attraction, because she had felt that before, or even a desire to know him better. Instead it was almost a feeling that she had come home, that she had finally found her safe place, and those feelings were dangerous.

Giving herself a mental shake, she admitted, "Thanks, I would appreciate that," and tried to put a bounce into her step to cover up the awkward situation and firmly shut down her emotional barriers. She could not afford to get invested in a stranger, and she didn't know if she would ever be able to trust a male again, not after …

"So," she continued, pushing her mind away from those thoughts, "what's your name?"

"Caleb," he responded, glancing down as they crossed the blue-and-white tiled hallway. "Caleb Rose."

"Nice to meet you, Caleb," she automatically replied. For a brief moment, she couldn't help but wonder if he was looking down her shirt as they walked, but refused to look at him to see. He was at least six inches taller than her, and she had unzipped her coat when she stepped into the warmth of the school. Ever since her experience with a former foster parents' son, she had been extremely careful never to wear revealing clothing, but she was also certain she had never stood beside a boy his height before either.

His last name registered in her head and she glanced up, relieved to see his eyes firmly ahead of them. "Really? Like the flower, or is it an old family name that is spelled differently but sounds the same?"

A deep chuckle caused the studded leather band around his neck to vibrate. "Yeah, like the flower. It's good for a laugh at least, and most people know better than to point out the irony."

Alyssa dipped her head in appreciation of both the irony and the information. "It could always be worse," she murmured, spotting the number on the door ahead and hoping they would reach the classroom before she would have to offer her name in response.

An elbow gently nudged her arm. "This is where you give me your name. Otherwise I'll be forced to call you new girl or give you a nickname of my own."

"Um ..." she stalled, then let out a sigh of relief when a teacher stepped into the hallway and pointedly looked at them. Though her jeans and Polo shirt sporting the school logo of a koala with boxing gloves gave her an air of casualness, her expression was stern and annoyed.

"Caleb Rose, you are late – again." Her voice was sharp, an indicator that this was an interaction they had on a regular basis.

A half grin spread on his face as he stepped across the threshold just as the final bell rang. "Or not."

A slight flush rose to her cheeks at the action, but she did not push the issue further. "Then go sit down. Now." Her chest rose slightly as she took a steadying breath and rolled her shoulders.

"Oh! You must be my new pupil!" Her hands clapped together in excitement as she beamed at Alyssa standing awkwardly inside the doorframe. "It is rather inconvenient to start when the first semester is already over, but we will do our best to make you feel at home and get you caught up in your studies. Come in, come in. There is an empty desk for you right over here. Welcome to English!"

Alyssa shuffled to the desk, carefully navigating through the narrow aisle and stepping over backpacks and over-sized purses. Not only was the desk in the center of the room, but it was also right in front of Caleb. She quickly melted into the seat, pulling out her new spiral-bound notebook and pencil before sliding her backpack under the desk and securing it between her calves.

The teacher, Mrs. Callen according to Alyssa's schedule, clapped her hands to quiet the classroom, smiling gleefully as she picked up her adjusted roster. Obviously, this was the highlight of her day, though

Alyssa knew it would be just one of the many annoyances in her own.

"Attention, class. Today we have a new pupil joining us. I want to make sure that she feels welcome and part of the Fighting Koala family. Please welcome, Alyssa ..." She glanced at her roster, brows furrowing before glancing toward where Alyssa sat with her eyes downcast. "Doe? Am I pronouncing that correctly? Alyssa Doe?"

She gave a sharp nod in reply. *Come on, teacher. Just read my name and start teaching, it's not that complicated*, she silently implored.

As the teacher turned to write on the white board, a girl with perfectly done curls turned around from two desks away and smiled coyly as her eyes inspected Alyssa. "Doe? Like a missing person? Are you a missing person, Alyssa, or just a female deer?"

Alyssa gave her a practiced smile along with her usual response. "Neither. It's just my last name."

The boy sitting in from of her turned around, Alyssa's body burning uncomfortably as his eyes raked over her face, causing her to squirm with the her lack of make-up, hastily brushed hair, and plain face. "You homeless? Sometimes that's the last name they give homeless kids around here, just so there is something for the record. I think that's the name anyway."

"If I was homeless, do you really think I would be sitting in school, ready to learn English? Can we start now?" She put as much venom into her quiet tone as she could muster. Her hands felt clammy where they rested on her lap, and she could feel her body heating as her heart began to race in her chest.

Not now, Alyssa, Not now. It was a fine line for her between self-defense and class disruption, and Alyssa had never been good at walking on a balance beam. That was how she ended up getting picked up by her social worker after her first day of school in the foster program. She had just turned ten, and had been extremely scared, bewildered, and hurt that her mom had dropped her off at school one day and then never picked her up.

For a while, she had been able to tell herself that her parents must be dead and that was why she was in the system. As she became older, she began to discover more information, and realized that her mom, flying solo since Alyssa was an infant and her dad left, had never died, she just dropped off her kid at school and kept on driving.

Six years later, and she still half-expected her mother to be outside of the school, full of apologies and wanting her daughter back. On the worst of the nights, she wondered if one day her father would pick her up and take her to live with him, even though he left when she was still in diapers. She asked her social worker about it once, but the woman had just shaken her head and said that he moved a long time ago, and was out of her reach.

So now she just hid all of the pain and bitterness deep inside where no one could find it, and heaped the coals over her own soul instead of using it to punish others for the hurt they inflicted with their words. Lashing out never did any good anyway. All it ever accomplished was another move, another bedroom, a new set of rules, and another awkward first day with the same stupid questions.

The classroom came back into focus as the gravelly voice behind her quietly contributed to the conversation. "Heck, I know if I were homeless you wouldn't catch me here. Obviously she just has an interesting last name." Caleb's voice became dangerously low and menacing. "End of story."

The immediate silence from the classroom startled Alyssa out the spiral of dangerous thoughts, and she looked back at Caleb gratefully. Caleb Rose, the goth punk rebel with a flower for a last name. If anyone knew what it was like to have a name you hated, it would have been him. If there was anyone who would know what she was going through, he was her best chance.

It was unfortunate that Alyssa knew what usually came along with punk kids, and was smart enough to never make the mistake of becoming close with one, again.

Two

Excited chatter bubbled around the cafeteria, filling Alyssa with dread as she tucked her backpack closer to her body and navigated her way to the lunch lines. Tables lined the center of the room, each a temporary island to the cliques and groups of students that had a very long-standing established order, a systematic society that was found in every school, developed over years and fiercely defended.

Fully suspecting that this would be the worst lunch she had come up against to date, because she knew from experience that small towns rarely lent well to newcomers, she built up the wall of indifference around her feelings. It was hard enough to fit in anywhere, much less a place where most of the kids had been in school together ever since kindergarten. No, Alyssa felt lucky to stay in a school for a semester, much less her entire life. Add to that the challenge of trying to fit in with a group of sixteen-year-olds who had completely different lives than hers, filled with the excitement of driver's licenses, cell phones, and dating, and lunch time was beyond stressful.

The line moved forward and she resisted the urge to pick at her fingernails, shredding the nails down to the quick. Her therapist told her it was a habit she had developed to "alleviate the nervous energy," but it never actually took away her nerves, and only resulted in jagged fingernails. Alyssa never had a manicure in her life and was never asked to come along when her past keepers had gone in for theirs, since it would have just been a waste of money on nails that would be destroyed.

Alyssa stepped up to the food counter and fought down the urge to dance in happiness. *Most teenagers would say this is slop*, she admitted as she approached the line, *but they have no idea how bad some shelter food tastes, or what it is like to be hungry and not know if there will be another meal*. She had been lucky in the foster family department, rarely having to go without food, but she still always worried about having enough, or eating too much.

School lunch gave choices, and that was something that kids like her were not used to having. While it may just be a choice between corn and peas, nuggets or pizza, it was still a choice, a small piece of her life that Alyssa could control without having any strings attached.

It was also a safe choice for her, one that would have no resounding repercussions later on. Her first foster mother had offered Alyssa choices as often as she could, but, having grown up in a household where children were seen and not heard, Alyssa froze every time her opinion was asked for consideration.

By the time she had wrapped her mind around the idea that she had a voice, a thought, a vote, her relationship with food had dissolved into one filled with stress and traps. She knew how much food cost; one foster couple had constantly fought about the price of food, so she ate as little as possible to keep the hunger at bay, so that she would not be a burden, and they would not have any reason to send her away.

One family, the one with the boy that Alyssa refused to think about anymore, would chuckle any time she gave her opinion on dinner. She would try to combine her favorite foods into one meal, never knowing when she would have the next chance to eat each item. So for her, an ideal dinner consisted of a slice of pizza served with mashed potatoes and cheesecake. They hadn't believed her when she said that was what she wanted, and she never offered her opinion in that household again.

At the end of the line were blue, plastic containers filled with ketchup, mustard, and mayonnaise, and Alyssa forced herself to walk by without pocketing an extra handful to save for later. While crackers and ketchup were nowhere near her favorite meal, it was something that was easily hidden, and enough to take the edge off when hunger became too distracting to get through the day.

The milk carton on her tray shook slightly, the result of her hands trembling as she surveyed the lunch room, hoping for an empty table. Most schools had one table that was empty, usually unofficially reserved for the roamers, those with lunch detention, or the kids who just never made friends. Her heart sank as she realized that this school was small enough that no extra table was available, and she was going to have to find another solution.

Just as she was debating asking the teachers on lunch duty if she could eat at their table, or pocketing the food and eating it in the safe privacy of a bathroom stall, her name was called from across the room. Her head turned toward the sound, and saw Caleb nod his chin in her direction, then at the empty chair beside him. Disbelieving, she looked around, certain that he must have been signaling to someone behind her in line. When she looked back his way his lips were twitching in suppressed laughter and he pointed at her, then down at the empty seat.

Huh, not the group I'd associate with him, Alyssa mused, hesitating in confusion before walking over. He was the only one at the table with a mohawk or any extravagant piercings, and was holding a conversation with a boy in a sweater vest. *Who wears a sweater vest these days?* The two guys next to him had their noses buried in a laptop as they ate, pausing briefly to point at the screen and chuckle. Across the table sat two girls dressed in running jackets and yoga pants, simultaneously scrolling through their texts and laughing as Caleb talked.

He patted the chair beside him as Alyssa approached, and she instinctively scooted the chair slightly farther away as she sat down and told herself to be brave.

Just for today, she reminded herself. *Just for today, I'll sit here and act like I have a friend, or might have a future*. Tomorrow she would need to figure out another seating arrangement, because she knew if she let herself get close to a guy like Caleb, her life would never be the same.

Three

"I trust you all had productive breaks," The math teacher's voice was tired, and the bags under her eyes were darker than they should have been for someone who had just come back from a holiday break. Her eyes trailed over the class, assessing the silent response, then she glanced down at a picture on her desk and smiled.

The gentle smile shot darts through Alyssa's heart and she focused intently on the cover of her notebook until the feeling passed. The keeper before her last had the same look in her eyes after she brought home her new baby, three days before Alyssa was picked up and taken away. It was the look of pure exhaustion and unwavering love. Some days Alyssa thought back and wondered if her mother had ever looked at her that way, but since she doubted it, she tried to move away from that train of thought whenever it crept into her mind.

Mostly she just remembered her mother as angry, stressed, and annoyed. Nothing Alyssa did could make her smile, or thaw the coldness. Always in the way, always needy, always wanting something; that was all her mother saw when she looked Alyssa's way. As she grew, Alyssa only saw a mother who wanted to be anywhere except standing in front of the little girl who loved her without reservation.

Mrs. Archer pointed around the room, calling upon people to relate the activities of their holiday breaks. This was the worst part of the year for Alyssa, having to figure out a story that was a completely believable lie. This year she couldn't figure out where to start, as she had just moved in with Miss Sona when the break started, and she knew nothing about this town or what to do in it.

Somehow Alyssa knew that if she said, "I spent my Christmas break moving into a total stranger's house after getting kicked out of my last house because both of the adults lost their jobs," she would be met with anything but sympathy. Her holiday did not involve any presents, family gatherings, singing, or happiness. It was just her, Miss Sona, and Darren, Miss Sona's fiancé, sitting at the breakfast counter in the apartment with platefuls of pizza.

She had wondered why it was just the two of them for the holidays; at least, until she came along. Both seemed incredibly friendly, the perfect kind of couple that family would want to invite over for dinner, yet they only had each other for the day. She quickly turned away from that mental pathway, knowing how quickly it could send her into a sense of total futility and bleakness, and tried to listen to the other teenagers relating their vacations.

An overly made-up girl with perfectly brushed blonde waves raised her hand. "Well, thanks to the economy, like, totally sucking lately, we could only go to Florida for three days this time instead of our usual full week. It was totally a bummer."

Alyssa made a mental note to stay away from that one. If going to Florida was her idea of a bad time, what would she think about spending every holiday in a room of awkward tension, surrounded by people whispering, "Is that the foster kid?" behind their hands.

"My vacation was awesome!" chimed the girl sitting behind her. "I was able to go skiing and snowboarding and then shop at all the cutest boutiques in the big city."

Mrs. Archer's tired eyes moved to Alyssa, and she felt her face grow clammy as she realized she was about to be called on and still had not developed her story. Who would she be this time? Which version of Alyssa Doe would fit in best at this school? Which *me* did she want to be?

A perky brown-haired girl beside her raised her hand, inserting herself into the teachers view and shifting her focus. Alyssa shot her a grateful look as she began to speak.

"Break wasn't too horribly exciting, but it was nice to get a break from homework. Oh, and I got to see some of my cousins from out-of-state. And open presents. And," she shrugged, "that's about it." Her eyes glanced Alyssa's way and she gave the tiniest of winks before adding, "How was your break, Mrs. Archer?"

"Oh, it was quite acceptable. Thank you, Brianna. Alyssa, how was your break?"

"It was okay," Alyssa answered, hoping that the drumming of her heart wasn't audible to the people around her. "I spent most of it moving here, and unpacking. Nothing too horribly exciting."

A snort from the front of the room had her lowering her eyes without thinking. A male voice filled with old-fashioned southern drawl filled the room. "Who moves halfway through the year? I bet you got kicked out of your old school or something."

Tears blurred Alyssa's vision as she desperately thought of a good response. She had never been good at comebacks, always thinking of the perfect response long after the moment had passed. Her eyes threatened to spill over until Brianna's voice sounded beside her.

"Oh please," she said curtly. "A lot of people move mid-year for normal reasons. Maybe her dad just got a new job assignment, or her mom got a promotion in a different area, or maybe they are military or government and her dad's job is to save your sorry butt from deadly threats." Her smile helped Alyssa's tears fade away.

"Government," Alyssa squeaked out, silently thanking her for giving the out that she needed. "It's not all that it's cracked up to be, that's for sure." The class laughed companionably as Southern Drawl rolled his eyes and turned back to face the whiteboard.

"Thanks," Alyssa whispered to Brianna.

"Don't mention it," she replied. "I just moved here last year and went through the whole, awkward first day thing, too. Jed's a grade-A jerk, so don't spend one minute worrying about any crap that comes out of this mouth."

Easier said than done, Alyssa thought as she tried to push the episode out of her mind and focus on the lesson, feeling slightly less alone.

Four

The scent of apple pie wafting through the air made Alyssa's mouth water as she stepped into Miss Sona's modest townhome, carefully removing her damp boots and placing them on the decorative river-rock mat beside the door. Being able to walk home had been a surprise and, along with pink cheeks and a clear head, it gave Alyssa time to think about her day and her situation.

While Alyssa still had had her suspicions for why a twenty-five-year-old, engaged, successful loan officer wanted to foster a sixteen-year-old girl, Miss Sona had been nothing but nice so far. Upon arrival, Alyssa had found a freshly cleaned bedroom, with soft sheets on the bed and a small empty dresser for all of her clothes.

Miss Sona had been genuinely shocked when the only thing Alyssa brought into her two-bedroom house was her backpack and small bag of clothes. Alyssa had always considered herself lucky that she had the backpack to hold her most valuable items, like her favorite book, therapy journal, and a picture drawn by one of her four-year-old foster siblings from several houses ago. She knew plenty of kids in the system that were moved in trash bags, their items gathered by the social worker while the child was at school or standing outside with a police officer.

She lost her favorite necklace the first time she moved, when the harsh reality of her new life came crashing down upon her head. Never realizing how easy it was for the foster parent to give her back, she had left her necklace at home because she didn't want to worry about it being broken at school. Then the white car picked her up from school, and she was dropped off at a new home, with a new family, and never saw the necklace again.

"Hi, Alyssa. How was your day?" Her newest keeper turned around in front of the stove and placed the pie on the counter, the source of the delicious smells of baked apples and flakey crust.

"It was okay, Miss Sona." Alyssa hung up her coat and slid onto a tall stool by the counter.

Jessica gave a little smile as she noticed Alyssa's rosy cheeks. "Did you enjoy your walk home? And please, call me Jessica. Miss Sona makes me feel so old."

"Very much, and I'll try." Gratitude filled Alyssa's voice as she responded.

She knew that it could not have been easy for Jessica to get permission for Alyssa to walk home, as most foster kids either relied on a special bus or rode with their foster parents to and from school. It didn't matter if you lived within eye-sight of the school; if you were a foster kid; you were considered a flight risk.

While Alyssa firmly understood the motivation for running, the need to escape, the need to regain some sort of control over your life, she could never take the step into running away. Life was terrifying and difficult enough already, she could only imagine how much worse it would be without a roof over her head, or an adult who at least pretended to care.

She had also seen what happened to children and teenagers after they try to run away, especially after they were officially labeled a flight-risk. Stricter curfews, even less privileges, long nights spent hiding out in tents, or being placed in public shelters, or even doing time in jail. Alyssa had a different path in mind for her life, and ending up on the streets was not going to help her live her dream.

When she entered kindergarten, the teacher had them draw a picture of what they wanted to be when they grew up. Alyssa wanted to train whales, to swim in the water with the majestic animals and teach everyone about how incredible they were. A little girl with big dreams, she had raced home to show her mom the picture and tell her all about her dreams.

But the divorce had already broken something in her mother, and all she saw in Alyssa's dream was the money for school and the employment uncertainty. Her mother impressed upon her that whale training was dangerous, and that Alyssa needed to focus on a safer path in life, like being a cashier at the local department store.

That night, her mom was talking on the phone and told her friend that she would be shocked if Alyssa did not follow in her footsteps, since she was already proving to be a strong-willed child. At five, Alyssa felt proud that her mom would want Alyssa to follow in her footsteps, to get married and have a child to care for and love.

By the time Alyssa was ten, she knew better, and while she had given up the dream of being a whale trainer, she knew she had better things in her future than a teenage pregnancy and apathetic future.

When Alyssa was twelve, she swore to herself that she would never follow the path of her mother, and worked tirelessly day after day to be smart enough, driven enough, so that she could be a success in life. She refused to be a mother who hated her children, wishing that they would have a mediocre life to ease the pain of her own broken dreams. She wanted so much more, and was determined to push beyond her mother's low expectations.

"Would it be okay if I went into my room to do homework?" Alyssa asked tentatively. A seemingly simple question, it had spurned suspicion and anger in the past, and she was not sure how Miss Sona, Jessica, would react.

Jessica just smiled and wiped her hands on the apron wrapped around her waist. "Absolutely. The pie will be ready to eat in about an hour, so I'll have a piece out for you when you are ready for a break."

"Thank you." Alyssa slipped off the stool and took her backpack into her room, leaving the door open so there were no questions about what she was doing.

Not that she ever did anything other than study, but she knew that kids her age, foster or not, tended to get in trouble behind closed doors. It was just easier to leave it open, and if she was truthful with herself, being in a closed bedroom was a claustrophobic nightmare ever since the incident with Jay.

She rolled onto her back on her bed and stared at the white snow slowly falling outside her window. It was hard to believe that only a year had passed since then, when she was fifteen and should have known better. Jay was the natural son of her seventh foster parents, and the most handsome guy she had ever met. Two years older than her, he immediately won her over with his funny jokes, courteous manner, and little waves when they were at school.

Alyssa was a girl full of fifteen-year-old dreams, dreams that had begun to bubble to the surface after spending six months in a house filled with laughter and happiness, and if there was a rule that doors had to remain open at all times, she assumed it was just because that's what was normal.

Then there was the night that his parents went out for dinner, leaving Alyssa alone with Jay, trusting that a babysitter would not be needed for the two teenagers, who assured them that nothing would happen and they would get to bed early.

At first, nothing did, and Alyssa enjoyed a night of pizza, crappy television shows, and being free from the watchful eyes of adults for two hours. Around nine, Alyssa said she was going to get to sleep, as she had to be at school early for a study group. Jay said he was just going to hang out on the computer for a little while, and would clean up the living room before his parents got home.

Alyssa had just drifted off to sleep when she heard her bedroom door click shut, and the noise was so foreign in a house where doors were to remain open that her eyes shot open immediately. Her body was so tense, so scared at the dark figure by her door, that she couldn't even form a scream.

Then her eyes focused, and she saw Jay smile as he put his finger to his lips, his chest pair and eyes glassy. "We still have about an hour before they get home," he whispered, grinning as he moved toward Alyssa, still huddled under the covers. "We won't do anything stupid or permanent, just play a little."

She could smell the alcohol on his breath, alcohol that could not have come from the kitchen, as both adults were very careful not to have anything in the house that the teenagers could use to get into trouble. He slid into bed next to her, and her body burned painfully from the warmth of his clothes against her skin.

Jay's hands slid under the covers, and her breath began to come in panicky gulps as they slid over her arms, bare as she only wore a tank top and shorts to bed. "Relax, Alyssa. You aren't the first girl I've been with, you know. This is all just totally normal."

Skin crawling, she quickly sat up and stumbled off the bed, only to find him moving with her. The knob of the closet door pressed into her back as he pressed himself against her. "Jay, no. If your parents come home, we will be in so much trouble."

"Not really," he whispered, hands once again exploring. "I would just lose my phone for a week; you would be the one in so much trouble, especially after they find the bottle of rum in my closet, you know, that you must have put there. That's why you had better just go along with it, so that everything will be fine by the time they get home. And if you say one little word to them about this, you will be back at the foster center and really screwed."

Tears coursed down Alyssa's cheeks as his hands continued to roam, and she felt frozen in fear, while her stomach burned with the thought that there was nothing she could do to protect herself. If she fought against him, she risked his parents walking in and misinterpreting her position. If she said anything, well, he made that threat clear enough.

So she stood silently in the darkness, focusing on the hard metal knob jutting into the base of her spine as she tried to ignore his hands on her body. With her eyes clenched shut, she didn't see the car lights as her foster guardians pulled into the driveway, so she didn't understand why Jay suddenly swore and spun her around. Knocked off balance, her arms closed over the nearest object, so when his parents flung open her bedroom door, it was to find her with her arms around him.

The social worker was there within half an hour, transporting a sobbing and confused girl to a temporary shelter for the night, while Jay smiled in the background. While her case worker, Patricia, seemed to believe her side of the story, she never heard if anything else came from it, and was placed in homes without teenage males to prevent anything from happening in the future.

Five

"Hey, Alli! Over here!" Brianna's voice carried over the lunch room, bringing a smile to Alyssa's face. While she had no intention to build a lasting relationship with the other girl, Alyssa had to admit it was nice having someone who was excited to see her during the day.

Alyssa plopped into the empty seat beside her new friend and tucked her backpack between her feet. "I didn't think math was ever going to end today."

Brianna laughed. "Yeah, no kidding. As if math wasn't hard enough to begin with, someone had to go and add letters to it. So not cool." She pulled a sandwich out of her lunch bag and took a bite. "Hey, what are you doing after school?"

With a shrug, Alyssa took a drink of chocolate milk, her latest vice. "Just going home and studying. Why?"

"Weelll," Brianna responded, drawing out the word. "My mom keeps pushing for me to redo my room, since I don't really have anything colorful or happy in it, and she's getting really sick of feeling depressed whenever she comes in there, so she was going to drive me to the mall, and I was wondering if you wanted to come."

"Oh." Alyssa fiddled with a chicken nugget and felt her body grow hot. "Um, maybe next time."

Brianna flicked the dew from the outside of her bottle of water across the table, lightly splattering Alyssa's tray. "Oh, come on. It will be fun. You study too much anyway. Caleb says all you do is go straight home after school and study." Her eyes crossed and her tongue stuck out of her mouth, giving Alyssa a clear picture of what Brianna thought of her lack of social life.

"I'd have to ask my … aunt," Alyssa improvised. No one would believe that Jessica was her mom, especially not in a town like this where everyone knew everyone and knew their nine-year age difference, but an aunt would be believable. "I'm staying with her while my parents finish up some business at our old house."

Brianna rolled her eyes. "Okay, so just call her and ask her."

Dry-mouthed and clammy, Alyssa mumbled, "I don't have a cell phone."

For a second Brianna just stared at Alyssa as if she had horns sprouting from her head, then reached into her purse and pulled out her phone, sliding it over the table. "That sucks. Here, use mine."

Alyssa picked up the phone carefully. She may not have a cell phone of her own, but she wasn't ignorant to technology, and she knew that this piece of metal and electronics cost more than the agency gave Jessica each month for fostering her. She pulled the small book where she kept Jessica's multiple phone numbers recorded and carefully dialed her cellphone number, feeling numb and frightened.

Jessica picked up on the second ring, and Alyssa had to clear her throat twice before she was able to squeak out hello. "I'm fine. No, nothing's wrong. Um. I was just wondering if it would be okay if I went to the mall with a friend, Brianna, after school."

Alyssa glanced up at Brianna, "She wants to know if she can have your mom's phone number?"

Brianna chuckled. "Ah, over-protective aunts. Here, let me talk to her. What's her name again?" She reached over and gently plucked the phone from Alyssa's grip. "Hi there, Miss Sona! Yep, I'm that Brianna. Still need mom's number?" She gave her the phone number and listened intently for a minute. "Absolutely! We'll see you for dinner then."

Eyes bugging out slightly, Alyssa stared at Brianna's happy face in disbelief. "Wait, she is joining us for dinner? I'm having dinner with you?"

"Yep!" Brianna grinned. "She said Darren is working late tonight, so it was just going to be you two for dinner, so she's going to meet us at the mall and we can all eat together. I've met her a couple of times, but I still can't believe that your aunt is so cool!"

"Yeah, she's pretty great." Alyssa dipped a French fry in ketchup and hoped the lie would not come back to bite her in the rear.

They ate in silence for a few minutes, listening to the din of the lunch room. Brianna finished her lunch first, zipping her fabric lunch bag closed and shutting her eyes momentarily. "I am so glad that it's Friday.

Are you going to the dance tonight? A couple of girlfriends and I are going together since we never have dates."

"Um, no. Not this time at least." Alyssa had never been to a high school dance. Most ended well after her mandated curfew, and they all cost more money than foster parents could, or would, afford. Add to it that permission slips had to have been turned in prior to her enrollment in the school, and she would be spending her usual Friday night at home.

The bell rang, and Alyssa settled her backpack onto her shoulders before placing her tray on the table set up next to the door. As they filtered out of the hallway she saw Caleb's tall frame heading over, and was surprised to see Brianna's eye roll.

"What do you want, trouble maker?" she asked, though her voice was light and there was a twinkle in her eyes.

He chuckled. "I haven't gotten my hug today. You know I can't stay out of trouble without my hug, so if I get into trouble today, it's on you."

"Oh, I suppose. Even though I'm still mad at you for doing the stupid crap I know you did last weekend." Brianna's words ended in a squeak as she was gathered into Caleb's arms and squeezed.

Releasing her, he turned to Alyssa. "How about you?"

"No," she whispered fearfully, taking a step backward and bumping into a student who gave her a nudge out of the way. Visions of Jay flashed into her head and she felt as if the lockers were closing in, preparing to squeeze her to death. A hand touched her elbow gently and she jumped sideways, wedging herself between the blue lockers and a black trash can.

"Hey, hey, hey. Easy, Alyssa." Caleb stood in front of her, hands at chest level and palms facing her in a gesture of surrender. "I may look scary, but I'm not going to touch you if you don't want me to. I don't roll that way."

Breathing in shallow gasps, Alyssa leaned her forehead against the cold locker for a second to get her bearings. After a moment, she turned back and tried her best to smile.

"I'm sorry I reacted that way. I'll see you after school, Brianna. Bye, Caleb." Alyssa merged into the crowd and disappeared, leaving Caleb and Brianna staring after her, confused and concerned.

"Your room has color!" Brianna spun around on the turquoise rug that now lay on the floor beside Alyssa's bed. While the mall trip had started out with the intent of re-doing Brianna's room, it quickly turned into a shopping trip for Alyssa.

It was the first time in her memory that Alyssa had been able to fully decorate a room of her own, to hang pictures or mirrors, and it was a little terrifying. Jessica had actually been the one who started it when she saw a display with beautifully beaded turquoise curtains that Alyssa had eyed longingly. Then Brianna and her mother discovered from Jessica that Alyssa's room had no decorations at all, and the teen was drawn into a triple tornado of decorating advice and enthusiasm.

"You didn't have to skip the dance for this, you know." Alyssa sat on the new stool with its purple and turquoise seat cover and looked at Brianna's reflection in the small free-standing mirror that now sat upon her dresser.

Brianna finished sticking purple flower decals onto the white bookcase the girls had put together earlier and grinned. "Of course I did! How are you supposed to grow and bloom in a room filled with gloom!"

Alyssa giggled at the bad rhyme and threw a pillow at her new friend. "Oh, shut up."

"You know I'm right. Now help me with these books!"

That had been Alyssa's happiest moment. Jessica had taken her into the bookstore and told her she could spend up to fifty dollars as a late Christmas present, and Alyssa now had her own little library.

Brianna organized the books on the case, cataloguing them out loud as she went, "*Change of Possession, Natural Selection, 15 Minutes, Control You.* You picked a pretty eclectic group here, you know." She studied the back of one. "*The Helping Hands* series sounds a little dark. Do you think I could borrow it when you're done?"

Alyssa just shrugged and looked up as Jessica appeared in the doorway.

"Would you girls like some snacks? I've got some chips and salsa in the living room."

"Sure!" Brianna's face lit up as she bounced to the living room.

Alyssa took a moment to stare at her room and feel joy before turning to follow Brianna. It was both strange and comforting to be surrounded by images and colors, reminders that she was just a teenager when she often felt so much older. Most of her rooms had simply been white, though sometimes with a few decorations that the adults felt a child or teenager would appreciate. Money was just as tight for foster families as it was for everyone else, so it made sense to keep the room the same for whoever needed the space, and Alyssa never begrudged them for the lack of decoration.

If anything, it made it easier when she left, not having anything that would be left behind to miss. She tucked her most anticipated book, *Fragile Creatures*, into her backpack, adding it to the small collection of items she could always call "mine." *A story about a girl who feels so alone she can't stand it. Hopefully she'll have the happy ending I probably won't*, she thought. *And I can't wait to read about giraffes.*

Jessica stood in the hallway, her eyes soft and expression sad. For a moment, Alyssa felt a pang of fear that Jessica was going to accuse her of stealing, after all, it was the woman's money that paid for the book.

Alyssa felt frozen to the spot as Jessica just walked over and looked around the room, a smile slowly growing on her face. "You girls did a great job in here. It looks so much better than it did when it was an office." She turned and tilted her head slightly as she took in Alyssa's rigid stance, eyes darting from the backpack to Jessica with barely concealed anxiety.

"Alyssa, I know your past hasn't been easy, but you are safe here. Everything in here is yours, for as long as you want to keep it. I will never take it away without your permission, okay?"

A quick nod and Alyssa felt her heart being wrenched by the treacherous feeling of hope. No one had ever said that to her before and the belief she felt hearing Jessica's words scared her. "Thanks, Jessica."

Seven

The day of her first test had Alyssa waking up with her stomach rolling and skin clammy. She was not prepared enough to do well, and she knew that, so she had asked her teacher about an extension. But Alyssa was already too far behind in the lesson, thanks to her late start, and the teacher needed for her to take the test with the rest of the class.

At least she said I could do a retake if I do too badly, thought Alyssa as she stepped into the classroom and slid into her seat. Her fingers tapped her pencil nervously on the plastic desk top and she felt her insides clench and twist as she worried more about the inevitable bad grade.

Glancing at the clock, she darted from her seat to the door and told Mrs. Callen she was going to use the restroom. Distracted by the violent ache in her gut, she didn't even realize she had left her backpack behind until she was washing her hands and walking back to class.

It will be fine, she told herself, willing the sweat that was beading on her neck to subside. *I just went to the bathroom, and it's safe in the classroom. There's no social worker here to take me away, so it will be fine.*

Her breathing hitched as she walked up to her desk and her backpack, once tucked under her seat, was nowhere in sight.

"Mrs. Callen," she asked, her voice shaking and breathing shallow, "have you seen my backpack? It was under my desk."

Mrs. Callen glanced her way, having just entered the classroom from her watchful position in the hallway. "No, Alyssa, I haven't. Are you sure you didn't leave it at home?"

Heart hammering in her chest, she felt flushed as she croaked, "No. I know it was in here. I always have it with me. It was under my desk."

The teacher gave her a smile of impatience and walked to the front of the room. "I'm sure you just left it in another classroom and forgot. Have a seat, Alyssa, and you can go to the office after class and check the lost and found bin."

"You don't understand," Alyssa pleaded, hearing her voice rise in desperation. "I have to have my backpack. It's important. Can I please go ask them now?"

"Alyssa Doe," her teacher's voice was sharp, her attention divided as she saw another student poking at the girl next to him with a pencil. "Dan Tyler, stop that this instant." She sighed heavily and picked up her white board marker. "You too, Alyssa. You can check in the office when you finish the test."

Alyssa sat, feeling nauseous and dizzy with the anxiety and fear that coiled through her body. A small note lay upon her desk, and, as she unfolded the paper, the room felt as if it had spun around in a wild circle.

Don't bother with the lost and found. It's gone for good. Too bad, so sad.

"Alli, you okay?" Caleb's voice hovered at the edge of her hearing as Alyssa's vision began tunneling.

She popped out of her chair. "I need to use the restroom again. I'm sorry." Stars floated in her vision and tears filled her eyes as she sprinted down the hallway toward the girls' restroom, stumbling over her own feet as she ran.

It was blessedly empty, and she made it to the corner before she felt her legs turning weak. Her back braced against the cold tile wall, she slid to the floor and wrapped her arms around her knees. The blood that pumped through her veins alternated between fire and ice, and her stomach dropped as the sloppily scrawled words refused to leave her mind.

The only thing she had from a time before she was in the system, the only item in the world that she was able to call her own, and now it was gone.

Sobs filled the room, echoing off the ceramic-covered walls and drowning any sounds from the hallway on the other side of the door. Her body shook violently as she took hiccupping breaths, trying to pull out of the dark spiral that was ripping and slashing at her self-control.

Her eyes drifted up, and she saw herself in the spotty bathroom mirror. Nothing but a tiny slip of a girl, too skinny to ever be pretty, too broken to ever be wanted, with a puffy face that was red from crying, surrounded by toilet paper tissues that she didn't even remember grabbing. Her mother had always told her that she would never amount to anything, and, for a moment, Alyssa couldn't remember why she bothered fighting so hard.

She had fought against the pain of being labeled a foundling, a child abandoned by perfectly capable parents. Then she fought against being labeled a troubled youth, trying so hard to be perfect all the time, to defy the role that society thought she should play. She fought against the emotions and hormones and yearnings that came with becoming a teenager, and had pushed everything that could possibly cause her pain or angst deep down into the black pit of her stomach, never to be felt again.

It bubbled up now, flooding her body with years of suppressed anger and resentment, heartache and yearning for a better life. She felt it course through her veins, sluggish at first, then moving lightning fast as she curled tighter and tighter into a ball, wedging herself into a corner as the stars in her view increased, and the fluorescent lights of the bathroom faded to gray.

Then something pressed onto her, a physical weight that supported her body, her head carefully cradled as her shoulders shook. The blackness within her heart fled as the feeling of safety and love surrounded her, as sudden and all-encompassing as if she had been tucked into a soft, warm blanket.

For a minute, she just let herself drift in the feeling of safety. No anxieties or fears could cross through the barrier around her, as if the unknown force had instantly erected an unbreakable shield around her heart and mind. Eyes still closed, she saw the black arrows of pain and doubt bounce off the shining walls, and felt the darkness recede.

"Alyssa, open your eyes. I have your backpack right here. Everything is okay now. Take deep breaths. It's going to be okay."

She shook her head, eyes clenched shut as her hand grappled around, finally closing in a death grip on the thin strap of her backpack that was placed in her lap. Her body wrapped around the bag and she sucked in a deep breath, aware of a warm body pressed against her side.

Hesitantly her eyes opened to slits and she looked at the blurry scene around her. Slowly, Alyssa's brain took in the silver-studded boots, black jeans, and solid chest that pressed against her side.

"There you are. Welcome back." Caleb's eyes were filled with concern as they took in her face, splotched red and pink, with the trails from her tears staining her cheeks. His arm was draped over her shoulder, pressing her closely against his body.

Instead of the touch filling her with fear, Alyssa found herself pressing closer against him, her head falling onto his shoulder as she remained curled around her backpack. His scent soothed her senses, an oddly comforting blend of cologne and cigarettes, and she felt her mind steadying as her emotional guards fell back into place.

As the reality of the situation pushed through the stuffiness of her head, she sat up quickly, craning her neck to look into his face. "You're in the girls' restroom!" she squeaked.

His response was a throaty laugh. "Yeah, well. You weren't coming out, so there was only one option." Caleb looked around and then winked at her. "It's much cleaner than ours, that's for sure." His free hand lightly brushed her tear-dampened hair from her cheek, tucking it behind her ear.

"What was that about, Alyssa? Those jerks didn't mean anything by it, and you scared the crap out of everyone with your response. It's kind of an unspoken thing here that when the new kid is accepted, their backpack or textbook or whatever gets hidden for the class. No one realized that it would freak you out like that."

The act of swallowing hurt, her throat sore from crying and her nose thick from the tears. Torn between the desire to continue hiding away her secret and the terrifying comfort of his arm across her shoulders, she found herself paralyzed with indecision.

Gentle pressure on her shoulder drew her back, and she took a deep breath before beginning.

"My dad left my mom and me when I was still a baby, and then my mom left when I was ten. She dropped me off at school one day and then just never came back. I never even told my social worker, but about a year later I found a note in a secret pouch in my backpack, this backpack, that told me exactly why."

Silent tears began to trail down her cheeks again, and Caleb sat in silence, his thumb gently stroking her shoulder. "She had me young, both of them did. They never wanted a kid, especially not as teenagers, but getting rid of me wasn't an option, so they thought they could deal with it. When her parents found out about it, they kicked her out of their house, and she moved in with her boyfriend and his parents. They had them get married to avoid the scandal, but it wasn't enough to keep them together. They let her stay there when he left until she was able to get an apartment of her own, and she tried to hold on, but it was just too much. So she just dropped me off and kept driving, to start her new life as a single, young woman in her mid-twenties with no strings attached."

Caleb swore softly under his breath, his jaw working as if he was trying to contain his anger, and she wondered briefly why he cared so much about two strangers throwing away their child without a care.

Alyssa pushed on with her story. "So, I went into foster care. I've been bounced from house to house, having nothing to call my own except this backpack. It's all I have, and if I age out of the system in two years, like I know I will, it may be all I will ever have that's really mine. When I thought it was gone … " her voice choked and she angrily dashed away her tears. "But it's not, and I would really appreciate if you wouldn't tell anyone about this."

Caleb sat shocked as Alyssa's mental gate crashed shut, causing her to jump up from the floor and walk over to the sink. She splashed some water on her face and took a deep breath. "I'm not special, Caleb. Not at all. Just pretend this never happened, okay? Just tell the other kids that I'm hormonal or high or something, but please don't tell them that I'm unwanted and broken."

He stood slowly, crossing the short distance between them in deliberate, smooth steps, as if approaching a wild animal. "Whatever you need, whenever you need it, I'm here for you, no matter what."

Alyssa jerked her head in a nod. "Thank you." She bit her lips as she saw the large spot on his shirt that was damp with tears. "And sorry for getting your shirt wet."

His lips just twitched into the half-smile of his, and he quietly replied, "Just give me advanced warning next time so I can bring a towel," before walking back into the hallway.

Eight

Graphite pencil in hand, Alyssa stared down at the blank canvas in front of her. The white expanse of space seemed like it was mocking her, compared to the beautiful pieces of artwork that were vividly displayed on the other canvases, projects halfway completed while hers had not even been started.

A shadow passed over her table as Mr. Burke stopped, then squatted down next to her. "I know this is probably tough, coming into the school year this late, and I want you to know, I understand. This project is meant for the entire year, but there's nothing we can do about that, so just give it the best you've got."

He straightened and gave her an encouraging smile as he rested his hand on the table. "I want you to focus on right now. Who is Alyssa Doe at this exact moment? What makes you happy? What makes you sad? Everyone is filled with colors, shapes, and hidden objects. Use that to begin this project, and then build upon it. I would like for you to come in during your study hall, just for ten minutes if that's all the time you have, and work on it. Find yourself and let the creativity flow."

Are all the teachers here so philosophical? She thought as he walked away, and then closed her eyes to search for inspirations. *What are my colors? What are my shapes?* Dwelling on who she was never led to good outcomes in the past. In fact, Alyssa made it a point to avoid thinking about where she was in life, preferring to only focus on where she was going.

Shapes, she thought, *what am I? A beanpole? A stick? An insignificant blog of goo?* She opened her eyes and looked around the classroom. The paintings were all so varied, some so realistic she thought they were photographs, others hints and suggestions of reality. A subtle glance at the canvas next to her revealed a painting filled with brightly colored lines, swirling around in a chaotic dance, with a straight line going through the middle, a staff where the lines met, regrouped, and swirled out again.

"What do you think?" The girl beside her gave a tentative smile and lifted her hand to scratch her nose, leaving behind a bright blue splotch of paint.

"It's incredible," Alyssa replied truthfully, before awkwardly gesturing to her nose. "Um, you have a little paint ... "

"I always do. My name's Carinna." Carinna giggled as she wiped at her nose.

"Alyssa. Nice to meet you." Alyssa suppressed a sigh as she turned back to her own canvas. She thought of the backpack incident, the memories bringing back every time over the last six years she felt scared, trapped, alone.

Her fingers moved, smoothly sketching on the canvas before her, and for once, Alyssa surrendered herself. Without thinking, the pencil danced over the center of the canvas, lightly sketching in the lines of a rosebud, tightly closed and surrounded by thorny vines, threatening to tear it to pieces if it ever tried to grow.

That's me now, she thought, placing the pencil on the table and standing up to go grab some paint from the tray on the supply table. *Colors, colors*. Hand on hip, she studied the available paint bottles and lightly bit her bottom lip. Finally settling on black, deep green, and a dark blue, she returned to her seat.

Once again, she let her hand flow, feeling herself sink into a state of almost eerie calmness as the brush moved over the canvas, placing the paint in tiny, precise movements. After forty-five minutes, the teacher cleared his throat, drawing the attention of the class and snapping Alyssa out of her mental vacation.

"That's time, folks. Please place your canvases on the tables in the back so they can dry and use the next ten minutes to clean up your supplies and stations."

Carinna glanced over at Alyssa and raised an eyebrow. "That's really interesting. It's almost like the thorns are protecting the little bud, saying, 'Stay away, bad things,' and waiting until it has time to grow into a beautiful flower and stretch to the sun. I love what you did with the colors. It would look awesome if you put a little beam of light on the tip of the bud. Well. Better go clean up now!" She gave another smile, picked up her canvas, and joined the students tidying their stations.

Head cocked to the side, Alyssa looked at the painting again, shocked by Carinna's interpretation of the thorns. She could see it though, both sides, the preventing and the nurturing. *Even my sub-conscious couldn't play by the rules*, she thought. Sighing, she put her canvas away and carefully cleaned out the brushes, returning them to the cup with her name written in masking tape so they would be dry for next time.

The bell rang just as she tucked her sketchbook into her backpack and joined the throng of kids in the hallway. Still confused by the labyrinth of the school, she lost time going the wrong direction in her quest to find her locker and arrived to her next class just as the tardy bell rang.

Caleb's seat was empty, and she couldn't help but give a sigh of relief that they weren't going to have to talk about the bathroom incident. She had successfully avoided him for the last two days, utilizing several excuses for last-minute restroom trips and clinging to Brianna, who seemed upset at Caleb about something and was actively snubbing him.

Those two mystified her, sometimes squabbling like siblings, other times as affectionate as a couple. Neither had a boyfriend or girlfriend, as far as she could tell, but they were such polar opposites that she would bet any attempt at a relationship would be over in a heartbeat. While Caleb seemed like a somber but fairly open book, Brianna was a mystery to her, often peppy and upbeat, but sometimes looking so lost and alone, but with a quick smile when she saw anyone looking her way.

"Thinking hard?"

Alyssa pushed the thoughts away as Caleb slid into the seat behind her. "Or hardly thinking," she said jokingly.

He chuckled. "Yeah, right. You're the definition of an over thinker. I could peg that from the second you had an internal debate on just saying hello to me."

Palms growing sweaty, she spun in her seat and saw the amused look on his face. "Listen, Caleb, about the other day ..."

Lips twitching, he grinned briefly before turning serious. "Don't mention it. We all have our moments. I'm sure you'll return the favor one day."

She turned her attention back to the front of the room as the teacher began to go over the objectives for the day. *Hopefully*, she thought, *I'll have a chance for that*.

Nine

"Alyssa, can I talk to you please?" Jessica's voice floated through the house to the bedroom where Alyssa lay on her stomach, propped by her elbows above her math book.

Slowly putting a pencil in the book to mark the page, she slid from the bed and took a deep breath. It had been two weeks since the incident at school, and Jessica had yet to bring it up. Every time that she called for Alyssa, she dreaded the conversation.

The school had to have called her, she thought as her thick socks padded softly down the short carpeted hallway. An outburst like that, of course a school would call the "parent" to make sure they knew their child was disruptive and unstable and should go to the crazy house.

She shook her head, her long, shaggy hair brushing her cheeks. *I can't think like that. Stop thinking like that*, she demanded to herself. Alyssa knew she was far from unstable, but when her brain constantly finding new things to worry about, it didn't take much for her to feel like she was falling into an abyss, to want to hide under her bed until the fears went away.

Jessica smiled as Alyssa walked into the room and patted the sofa seat beside her in invitation. Her body was tucked under a thick, crocheted blanket, and her hands were wrapped around a mug of hot chocolate.

"You okay, Alli? You're looking a little green?" Her brow furrowed slightly as she watched Alyssa sit down, seeing the way her throat moved as she rapidly swallowed, and the thumbs systematically shredding the nails on each hand.

"Yep, just doing some math homework. Um, you wanted to see me?" Alyssa struggled to keep her voice even, then tucked her hands between her knees and shut her legs, trapping her hands from giving away her nerves.

Jessica took a long sip of hot chocolate, then nodded to the counter. "There's a cup for you too. I was thinking, would you like to take a trip to the mall? Maybe take Bri with us? I have a few things to pick up and thought you girls could use some retail therapy."

Relief flooded Alyssa's body. "Okay. Can I borrow the house phone to call her?"

An odd look, then Jessica replied, "Of course you can. Alyssa, it's your phone now too. I mean, don't be calling any boys in Mexico or anything, but you don't have to ask if you want to call Bri." She took another sip. "Is there anyone else you want to invite?"

"No," Alyssa answered too quickly, forcing a smile to cover up the awkwardness. Even though she had been trying to push Caleb out of her life, he was like a puppy, always attached to her side. She almost lost it when he walked her home the day before and Jessica saw them together. Her keeper had greeted him warmly, but who knew what she was thinking about Alyssa having someone like him as an influence. While she was very careful to never be around him when he had been engaging in activities that would get her in trouble, just the association had her paranoid.

"Mhm, okay then. Go give her a call." Jessica looked as if she were holding back a smile as Alyssa moved toward the phone cradle on the kitchen counter.

A few minutes of barely contained excitement later, Alyssa was back on the couch and trying hard not to grin. "She said she could be ready in fifteen minutes, if that works for you."

Jessica stood and stretched, arching her back and groaning at the creaks and pops. "I officially sit too much. Do you want to start doing something together? Maybe horseback riding or hiking or something?"

"Um, whatever you want," Alyssa stammered. She had always loved horses, but never had the opportunity to be around them. Hiking, or any sort of outdoor activities for that matter, had always been out of the question, as they could cause injury or allow her to bolt, not that she ever would.

"Well, why don't we wait until after your school trip to Bayberry Therapeutic Equine Center, and then we can see if we want to start volunteering there together? You still have a few days to turn in the permission slip, so you should be okay." Jessica's face was turned toward the floor as she tied her black sneakers, and after a moment of heavy silence, she looked up to see Alyssa's stricken face.

"Alli, sweetheart, what's wrong?"

Alyssa took a deep breath and blinked back tears. "I'm sorry. I know I can't go on field trips like that. It's too dangerous and costs too much and I didn't want to bother you by giving you the form and now it's way too late to get the approvals." Her mouth clamped shut, aware that holding back information about school was considered insubordinate in a lot of households. Her eyes dropped down, staring at the chocolate brown carpet beneath her feet.

"Hey, it's okay." Jessica slowly crossed the distance between them and gently tapped Alyssa's foot with her own to get her attention, having learned early on it was the only touch the teen seemed to be able to tolerate. "Your teacher, Mr. Sanders, came by the bank and mentioned it, so I thought I'd remind you. Do you not want to go?"

"I do," Alyssa said quietly, adding, "more than anything," in a soft whisper.

"Well, then, I don't see what the problem is." Jessica smiled and Alyssa felt a small grin flit across her own lips.

It was a short ride to pick up Brianna from her house, then a slightly longer one to reach the mall that sat thirty miles out of the small town. After confirming that Brianna had her phone on and fully charged, Jessica dropped off the girls at the entrance and went to park the car.

Brianna turned to Alyssa as they stepped just inside the doors, warm air blasting away the frigid outdoors. "Still nothing about school?" Caleb had told her everything that happened, while Alyssa quietly sat beside the pair at lunch, staring intently at her food and wishing everyone would just stop talking about it.

Alyssa shook her head quickly, eyes scanning the doors. As new as Jessica was in her life, she was beginning to feel a small level of trust creeping into her heart, despite her best efforts to tamper it down. *She's just another keeper*, she told herself sternly. *Don't let yourself like her or you're going to get hurt.*

That was what happened at her favorite home. She was thirteen when she moved in with the Herbergers, and full of changing hormones, anger, and a deep sense of guilt. A childless couple in their late forties, the Herbergers had been the closest thing to a normal family that Alyssa could hope for. With their sprawling, tidy, but not pristine, colonial home that was always filled with the smells of baked goods or hot dinner, she felt immediately welcomed, immediately loved.

At that age, she had not yet been jaded to the system, had not experienced enough rejection and movement to become the untrusting person she knew she was now, and she melted into their love. Homework help came every night, Mrs. H. patient and caring as she walked Alyssa through math problems that gave her trouble, though they were basic for every other child her age. Weekends were spent with trips to the local playground, apple orchards, or just taking long rides in the car and listening to silly songs on the radio. Bedtime was filled with joy instead of fear, with the woman she had come to love as a mother always tucking her into bed, reading stories, and then kissing her forehead goodnight.

Six months later, it all fell apart. One day, Mr. H. came home before Alyssa had left school, and when she arrived both adults were standing at the bus stop, Mrs. H surreptitiously wiping tears.

He stayed home after that day, waking up before Alyssa went to the bus and disappearing into his luxurious home office, while Mrs. H. always seemed on the verge of crying. Meals became slimmer, and weekend trips stopped. She could hear them arguing at night when they thought she was asleep, catching her name but never what was being said.

The last day with them, she stepped off the bus, full of exuberance and glee that she had received an A on the math test that Mrs. H. had been helping her study for over the last month, and found her world turned upside down.

They were both standing on the front step, Mrs. H. openly weeping, while Mr. H. had an arm wrapped around her shoulder for support. A beat-up white car was parked in the drive, and Alyssa felt confused and a little frightened that her new case-worker from social services was standing beside it.

Patricia moved forward, a look of worry on her face when Mrs. H. pulled herself from her husband's grip and wrapped her arms around Alyssa's small body, tears dropping onto Alyssa's hair. Mr. H. followed her, dropping down to one knee and wrapping them both in his arms.

"I'm so sorry. This wasn't the way things were planned. I'm sorry. I tried to find another job, but there's nothing out there. I failed us all. I'm so sorry." He gave Alyssa a kiss on the forehead, and led his wife back into the house.

Anger and a deep feeling of loss ripped through Alyssa as the social worker held open the passenger side door of the white car and helped the young girl buckle her seat belt.

"Alyssa Doe, I want to make something clear." Patricia's voice was firm but tired as she waited for Alyssa's small brown eyes to shift upward. "This is not your fault. None of it is your fault." Her voice cracked on the last two words and she turned the key in the ignition, driving Alyssa away from the only place she felt truly loved.

Ten

Alyssa stood in the bathroom for a moment, staring at herself in the mirror. Jessica had finally acquiesced to trimming her hair, and she slightly turned her head side to side as she took in the way the shorter cut caused a natural curl to wind into her hair. Having the tips touch her shoulders was a new feeling, as it usually was tied up into a ponytail or messy bun, but Alyssa found herself enjoying the way it softly draped on her skin.

Dressed in soft fleece pajamas, she opened the door and headed into the hallway, pausing momentarily as she heard Jessica's voice talking angrily to a person on the other end of the phone.

"Yes, I understand the protocol, but I was just informed of the field trip." A long pause. "No, I do not have any fears of her running away, or getting hurt. They will be indoors and supervised at all times and I know and trust the lead teacher." Another pause, and Alyssa crept down the hallway, feeling sweat bead on her forehead as she moved as close to the living room as she dared, while still remaining out of sight.

"Look, Pat, I appreciate the history you have with Alyssa, and I know that this is quick, but I really think this trip would be good for her. I have known the teacher personally for many years, and Alyssa will be in no danger. The form has the liability waiver and I will sign off that I will not hold the center, the school, or you guys liable if something were to happen to her. I'm willing to front the cost of the trip myself, so I just need to get the paper signed off so she can leave the school with all of the other kids."

A thread of hope wound through her chest. She might be able to go on the Bayberry trip, a trip, any field trip, just like a regular student.

"Okay, I'll fax them over in the morning. Yes, the field trip is on Friday. Yes, you can feel free to call Alyssa if you want to talk to her about it. Is there anything else you need from me?"

Alyssa slid her head so that she could see Jessica through one eye. Her keeper paced the kitchen with the cordless phone, her face becoming more and more strained, her body tense and her voice rising. "What do you mean, Darren called you? No, Patricia, I can assure you that everything is fine. Alyssa is not too much trouble at all, so I'm sure he must have been mistaken when he told you I was stressed."

Jessica's hand drifted to her head, pulling her hair half out of the plastic clip as her fingers tugged at the roots. "Of course it's an adjustment, but we're doing fine. She is developing friendships and really starting to get on her feet. And," her voice developed a very no-nonsense tone again, "that takes me back to my original point. I will send you the field trip information tomorrow morning. Thanks for your help."

Alyssa held her breath as she tip-toed back to her room and sat down in front of her new vanity. She hadn't seen much of Jessica's fiancé, Darren, since moving in, but had assumed that was just because of the two adults' busy schedules. That tiny thread of hope grew fragile and thin as she thought back to the conversation.

An adjustment? Understatement of the year, she thought bitterly, walking over to her window and pressing her forehead gently onto the cold glass pane. She was so busy learning to enjoy life that she forgot this was all just temporary. Of course, it was going to be temporary. Jessica and Darren would get married, and want to move in with one another. *Had they lived together before I came along*, she wondered, *or did I delay that action?* It was not common for unmarried couples to be able to foster a child, and would explain why Darren was less than welcoming toward her.

They would want to have their own kids, their own pets, their own life. What young couple in their rights minds would want to limit their life by keeping her around?

Alyssa felt a tear slide off her cheek and closed her eyes, counting her breath as she steadied her mood. A chime sounded from behind her, the sound so alien and out of place in her quiet bedroom that she jumped, her heart rocketing into her throat.

The light purple cell phone sat on her nightstand, buzzing away, walking across the nightstand as it vibrated a little dance. She caught it just as it dropped from the edge, smiling momentarily as she thought, *I have a cell phone.*

Jessica had set it up in Alyssa's name, though she had to co-sign to open the account. It was not the fancy phones that all of her classmates had, for Alyssa could not stand the stress of knowing she was carrying around something that expensive, but it still made her giddy. She had a phone, hers, something in her name that she could keep on her person and take with her no matter where the white car drove her. All she had to do was figure out how to pay for it, but at seven dollars a month and with a year's worth of loaded minutes, she was sure she could find a way.

It started chiming again, and Alyssa looked down in confusion as the tiny words "Message – Caleb" flashed on the tiny display screen. She flipped it open and took a minute to figure out how to open the message, thinking she was the only teenager in the world who did not instinctively know how a cell phone worked.

Welcome 2 fone world. Now U R stuck with us 4eva! Cya at school

Even though her eyes rolled at the text speak, her lips began to twitch of their own accord, pulling tightly upward until her cheeks ached with happiness. Then the giggles started, the sheer relief that this time she could stay connected to her friends, and Alyssa spent the rest of the night figuring out how to reply.

Eleven

The scent of earthy hay and well-oiled leather enveloped Alyssa as she stepped across the wooden beam of the barn entrance. Her class filled in the spaces around her, all fifteen students standing in jeans and tennis shoes, their hooded sweatshirts and coats pulled tight against the chill of the outside air. They gathered in the entrance to the barn, speaking in hushed tones as the owner of the Bayberry Equine Therapy Center closed the wide, double doors behind them and stepped to the front of the group.

"Welcome! My name is Wendy and I'm the owner and founder of the BETC. We are so happy to have you here today. We are going to start off the day by watching a short video on what we do here, and then put you strong youths to work so you can earn some community service hours for your future diplomas. Follow me!" Wendy turned, her blonde ponytail bouncing with her enthusiasm as she led the group through the barn and into a small meeting room.

Alyssa sat down and tucked her backpack between her knees, watching the video in rapt fascination. She had no idea that horses could be used for therapy, or how effective the beautiful animals could be for people suffering from a variety of physical and mental ailments. When a mother came on the video talking about how her child said his first word at the age of twelve, and the word was "horse," it brought tears to her eyes.

After the video, Wendy took the group through the barn for a brief introduction to the horses. Ranging in size from a tiny miniature pony whose back only came up to her hips, all the way to a long-legged Thoroughbred with a white blaze down his face, every horse had a purpose and role at the center.

"This here is Cheeky," Wendy cooed as she reached over the stall door and gave the bay Miniature Horse a rub between the ears. "We don't use him for riding, but his special job is helping the littler riders and visitors feel more comfortable around horses."

They slowly walked down the hallway, Alyssa occasionally lifting her hand to rub a velvety muzzle as she passed. At the end of the long aisle sat a collection of rakes, hay forks, and buckets.

Wendy clapped her hands gleefully. "Alright, so your first job of the day is going to be cleaning out stalls. Totally exciting, am I right? The ones over on this side are horse-free, so we are going to start there. Just scoop the hay fork under the soiled sawdust, and then put it into the bucket. When the buckets are about half-full they go out to the large trailer in the back, to be put into a giant compost pile and turned into prime fertilizer."

One by one the students reluctantly went up to gather the tools and head into the horse stalls. While Alyssa was dubious about the quality of work that the center would get out of the reluctant teens, most of whom were girls who had expected something a little more fun out of this trip than cleaning up poop, she knew they would put forth a good effort on the surface.

That was because everyone in the class except for Alyssa, even including Brianna, had a major crush on their teacher. *Well, all the girls anyway*, she amended in her head. She could certainly understand why Mr. Sanders' chocolate brown hair and sea blue eyes drew attention, but she refused to let herself be charmed by his smile or easy-going attitude. Really, she refused to let herself be charmed by anyone.

"What'cha thinking about?" Caleb's voice sounded from just beside her shoulder, causing Alyssa to jump and emit a short, highly pitched squeal.

"How many times have I asked you not to sneak up on me?" Alyssa turned and glared at him, her hands sliding to her hips as he just looked at her bashfully.

"About one less time than I've done it." Amusement and affection filled his voice as Alyssa rolled her eyes. "I just wanted to point out that you actually got assigned a stall with a horse in it, and if you don't get in there, someone is going to steal it away."

"Oh, well then, thanks. You want to haul away my bucket once I'm done?"

His snort gave her the answer, and Alyssa shook her head as he walked down the aisle to help Brianna. Puzzlement fell upon her face as she watched the horses' reactions to his presence, every single one stretching their heads out into the aisle to gently lip at his mohawk, or nudge his shoulder.

The smile that flashed when each horse made contact was one she rarely saw. She was used to his many smiles, the sarcastic one, the humorous, the sadistic, but this look of pure joy and peace was one she knew she would treasure. His hands gently touched each horse, scratching ears, caressing cheeks, and tickling whiskers.

She ducked into the stall when he began to turn toward her, wanting to give him his moment of unencumbered peace.

A soft flutter of breath came from the corner of the stall, where the inhabitant had wedged himself. One of the strangest horses she had ever seen, he was the color of light caramel, and had a stiff mane of white with black tips.

Her hand slid toward his body of its own accord, fingers stretched to gently caress his soft, velvety muzzle. The horse just looked back at her with big, empty, brown eyes, an expression she saw every time she looked in the mirror.

"What's your story, handsome guy? Why do you look so lost and alone in this happy barn?" Her voice was a quiet whisper, and the horse merely flicked one of his ears her direction before releasing a loud sigh and repositioning his forehead into the wooden corner of the stall.

Wendy gave a quiet cough and leaned her arms on the top of the stall door. "Lost is a good word for him. Yuda was one of our best horses, the one we always saved for the riders with the most crippling of issues, both physical and mental. There was one little girl, Amelia, who had been coming here for the last eight years, and always picked him to ride.

"They were a perfect match. He was her steady, reliable rock in a world filled with chemotherapy, experimental medication, and far more pain than any twelve-year-old should bear. Together, they worked to move her out of her cage and bring out the best of her situation."

Alyssa gently stroked the stiff, bristly mane. "What happened to her?"

"She lost the battle, two weeks ago. Her mom came to give us all a picture Amelia drew of Yuda and let us know that she wouldn't be coming back. Yuda saw the mom come in, and started prancing around in his stall, snorting and nickering like he always did when Amelia and her mom came to visit."

Wendy bit her lip and let out a deep sigh, fingernails picking at the wooden door below her hands. "She couldn't even look at him, understandably, I guess. He was a reminder of the daughter she had lost, the brilliant light that had been taken from all of us for absolutely no reason that we could fathom."

Both stood silently after that, the adult trying to pull herself back together while the teen let herself sink into the reality of a situation worse than hers.

"I was left behind too," Alyssa mumbled, fingers brushing at hay that had fallen into the horse's mane. "My dad left when I was little. Mom said that he made a new family, that he didn't like ours anymore so he left and started over. They were married long enough to give me his last name, but I never knew him, and have never been given a chance to meet him." Her breath quickened, and she hated the trembling that exposed how the words and memories still hurt. But the look in Wendy's eyes was one of empathy and understanding, and the words just seemed to flow of their own accord.

"Then, when I was ten, my mom left me at school. Just, dropped me off as usual, and never came back. For three hours, I sat in the principal's office, insisting, hoping, that she was just running late, or got stuck in traffic, or maybe the car broke down and she was getting our neighbor to help. After the third hour, the school had to call the police. They picked me up and took me back home, prepared to find a mom who had just become distracted and would be grateful that I was okay."

The horse moved his head slightly, his broad cheek coming to rest on her shoulder. She moved her hand to rub the wide space between his eyes, lost in her memories.

"She wasn't there though. The house was dark, the car gone, the garage door still open, and the front door unlocked. One of the cops stayed in the car with me while the other one went in to see if something had happened, if there was any danger, I suppose. After a few minutes he came out, and they both took me inside. Her closet was empty, her dresser, and the kitchen too. Like, she just threw everything in the car and then left once it was full. They grabbed a few trash bags, since I didn't have a suitcase and I couldn't fit much in my backpack, and told me to pack some clothes, because I couldn't stay there by myself."

A tear rolled down Alyssa's cheek and she buried her face in the soft fur of the horse's cheek. "At least his person didn't leave by her choice. My parents just left me. They knew exactly what they were doing, and left me anyway."

She looked up at a sharp gasp from the aisle, and found Brianna hovering at the stall door, quietly crying for her friend. "Alli, I had no idea."

Alyssa gave a weak smile, her automatic reaction to stress. "Now you know why I'm so screwed up. Why I can't risk being seen with the wrong person or doing badly in school or be anything less than perfect. I'm already a person no one wants, so I have to make sure they don't have any more reasons to get rid of me."

For a moment, a sniff was the only sound in the barn, then Brianna was in the stall, her arms wrapped tightly around Alyssa. It was like Brianna knew that Alyssa need to feel loved, connected to someone else in the world.

"We want you. Your aunt and Caleb and me. Screw your parents. They don't deserve you if that's the kind of people they are. We'll be your family now, forever and ever."

A harsh laugh caused the horse to jump slightly. "Jessica isn't my aunt. I lied to feel just a little more normal. She's just my newest foster guardian, my newest keeper. When she's tired of me, I'll be out the door and never see any of you again."

Brianna squeezed her tighter as Wendy left to find Mr. Sanders. "Not this time, not anymore. This time you have us, and we're not letting you go without a fight."

Twelve

A quiet knock at the front door broke Alyssa's tenuous slumber, and she rolled over to blink at the clock. She rubbed her eyes, certain that she was still dreaming, because it was past eleven and the house rule was that everyone was up for breakfast by 7:30am on the weekend, no exceptions.

A second knock sounded, and she bolted out of bed, flinging on the jeans she had worn yesterday and quickly pulling a short-sleeved shirt over the sports bra she always slept in. *How did I sleep so long?* She chastised herself. *Mrs. Hallaton is going to be livid.*

Hand gripping the doorknob of the half-opened door, her brain finally woke up enough to look around, and take in the photos taped to the door.

Alyssa and Brianna, grinning in matching pajamas with their hair sticking up like puff-balls after a sleepover.

Alyssa, Brianna, and Caleb, taken in the middle of lunch from Caleb's cell phone and printed on Brianna's special photo-printer.

Alyssa petting Yuda, a rare, unguarded smile upon her face.

I'm not there anymore, she thought as her forehead slowly dropped until it rested upon the white, wooden doorframe. *That was a different house, a different life.*

Footsteps sounded in the hallway and she fully opened the door to find Jessica standing, hand poised to knock against the frame, looking like she just rolled out of bed herself in her dark blue yoga pants and loose black tank top.

"Hey, Alli. Some neighbor kids were selling cookies, do you want some? I was just coming to see if you were up and wanting some breakfast when they knocked. You okay? You seem a little out of breath."

"I'm fine, and no thanks." She stepped out of the room, being sure to leave the door wide open for the informal inspection all of her foster keepers needed to perform. "I'm sorry I slept so late. It won't happen again."

Jessica gave a chuckle and walked down the hallway toward the kitchen. "Oh, please. When I was your age you couldn't drag my butt out of bed before noon unless you dropped water on my head. Which my mother did. On many occasions. Don't worry about it. You obviously needed some sleep. I saw your desk light on late last night."

Chills ran down Alyssa's arm. "I was just studying, I promise. It won't happen again."

Jessica turned, her eyes searching Alyssa's as she lightly took her hand. "Alli, you know I don't mind you staying up late as long as it doesn't interfere with school. What's wrong?"

"I just, it's just," Alyssa stammered, her heart pushing to confide in this woman who seemed to really care, whose eyes told Alyssa that she was not just saying the words. "Lost in a memory, I guess."

They reached the kitchen, and Jessica took a moment to make herself a cup of coffee, and Alyssa a cup of hot chocolate, before asking, "Do you want to talk about it?"

Alyssa wrapped her fingers around the warm mug and stared at the green laminate counter. "I don't know."

"If it helps," Jessica busied herself at the stove, flipping pancakes in one pan and laying bacon in another, "I do know a bit about your past." Hands full, she blew a loose strand of hair out of her eyes. "Your record included the rules from the Hallaton House, and I was a bit shocked at that, especially given your exceptional behavior for all of your guardians."

"They made sense," Alyssa mumbled, eyes glazing as she became lost in memories.

The Hallaton House had been the biggest shock. Her sixth or seventh house, she had lost track by that point, the Hallaton House was a group home for foster children when no individual household placements were available. Set up to accommodate four male children and four female children, the house was run with a strict set of rules.

Breakfast was mandatory, and you had to be fully dressed and at the table by 7:30, no exceptions. All children were in their rooms at seven pm, and motion sensor alarms had been set up at the end of each hallway that would sound an alarm if a child crossed from their hallway into the main living area. Each hallway consisted of two bedrooms, with two children in each, as well as a bathroom.

Lights out was at eight, with random checks by the guardians until around ten-thirty. For Alyssa, that had been the hardest part. By then, she had already fallen behind in her school-work, and her new high school workload was impossible to complete by lights-out, especially when she had to complete her daily house duties as well.

Each child was responsible for keeping the room tidy, clean clothes in their shared closet, and dirty clothes in individual hampers. Any toys, books, or clothing left on the floor after they left for school was confiscated by the house mother, regardless of how long the child had possessed it. Every child was expected to pick up after themselves, assist with cooking dinner, and clean-up. Hampers were brought to the laundry room every Wednesday and Sunday, and the clean clothes had to be put away before bed that night.

Then there was assisting with the yard work, helping with the younger children, and bi-weekly meetings with the family counselor. Showering or bathing, picking out clothes for the next day, vacuuming, dishes, and dusting were other activities that, while necessary, took away time from studying.

Living at that house had given Alyssa a firm understanding of the need for perfection, and what would happen when it wasn't achieved. One girl had stayed there for only two days before she refused to bring her laundry hamper to the laundry room. The next day, the white car was waiting when they got home from school. The Hallatons tolerated nothing but the best behavior, and made it clear that if you were not going to give them the best, they would replace you with another child who stood a chance at redemption.

"None of us stand a chance," Alyssa mumbled as she pushed her eggs around.

Jessica looked up from her plate, but remained silent, giving Alyssa time to process her thoughts.

"The rules made sense," Alyssa said, glancing up at Jessica, the lack of surprise on the woman's face confirming that some of the memories had fallen from Alyssa's lips as she relived the past, along with reading Alyssa's records. "I get it, especially now. The alarms were to make sure no one snuck over to the other bedrooms, or tried to run away. A couple of the teenagers tried, because they were lonely, I guess. They didn't even realize when Jenna did it, because she disabled the alarm, but a month later they found the pregnancy test she stole from the pharmacy and questioned the boys ... and yeah. The obsession with cleanliness and order a necessity, because with eight children in a house, things would become chaotic so quickly. They were trying to teach us about responsibility and life the best way they knew how."

She felt a tear trickle down her cheek and rubbed it away angrily. "But I was just fourteen. I wasn't trying to be bad when I set off the alarm. I just had a nightmare and was so scared. They didn't believe me though, and thought I was trying to sneak out, so they sent me away the next day."

"Do you still have nightmares?" Jessica's voice was soft and low, her gaze on Alyssa's hand holding the fork, the trembling vibrating the eggs where it rested.

Alyssa nodded. "Every night. They all start the same way. The police car comes for me, and ... " The words were strangled, as if her heart was pushing them out, while her head was forcing them back in. Confessions were dangerous, ammunition to use against you in group therapy, proof that you were not right in the head and needed more intensive care, institutionalized care.

"Alli." Jessica's hand slipped over Alyssa's where it lay on the table, still shaking like a leaf. "My door is always open, no matter if it is day or night. You don't have to be alone in the darkness anymore. I'm here now, and forever."

Thirteen

Caleb's red truck pulled in front of Jessica's house and beeped, prompting Jessica and a flustered Alyssa to exit the front door.

"Come on, you two. Time to go!" Caleb had moved out of the mohawk phase and his short ponytail fluttered in the light breeze as he opened the passenger door to his truck.

"Caleb?" Alyssa turned from Jessica to Caleb, a perplexed look on her face as she climbed into the passenger seat of Caleb's truck and Jessica headed to her own car.

"That's my name, babe, don't wear it out." He gave Alyssa a wink, and steered the truck onto the main road.

A glance in the side mirror confirmed that Jessica was following behind in her little blue sedan. Her keeper gave a little wave and Alyssa waved back before focusing on the road ahead.

"So ... where are we going?" Alyssa fidgeted with the hem of her jacket, uneasy with being escorted to any vehicle with no knowledge of the destination.

There was no reply as Caleb turned onto a different road, carefully watching his speed for once, aware both of Alyssa's safety as well as Jessica's opinion of his driving. "It's a surprise."

She rested her arm on the door and stuck her tongue out at him. "Okay, then tell me, how do you and Jessica know each other well enough to make a surprise for me?"

That brought a chuckle from him. "Small town, Alyssa. Everyone knows everyone here."

"And yet she still lets me hang out with you?" The words fell from Alyssa's lips before she realized it, and she flushed bright red as she tried to make herself smaller in the seat. "I'm sorry. That sounds horrible. I didn't mean it to sound like it did. Crap. Caleb ... "

He sat quietly a moment before shrugging. "To be perfectly honest, I don't get it either. I know I wouldn't trust a young woman in my care around a guy like me."

"Young woman in your care? Ugh. That sounds so stuffy."

His fingers tapped anxiously on the wheel as he turned another corner. "Well, how would you say it? How would you describe you?"

"A foster kid," Alyssa said quietly. "Foundling. Baggage Girl. Guinea Pig Kid. Mistake." Her tone grew increasingly bitter with every word.

The truck came to a smooth stop in a parking space and Caleb reached over, tweaking Alyssa's hair. "I like my phrase better, stuffy or not. I don't know what a foundling is, but you are not baggage, and you are certainly not a guinea pig kid or any kind of mistake."

"Oh really? Then why else would a twenty-five-year-old want to take care of a sixteen-year-old screw up whose own parents didn't even want her?" Alyssa glared out the window, equally upset at the situation and her outburst. She never lost control, not after she saw what happened to children who mouthed off, even to other children in the foster home. But there was something about Caleb, the way he pushed at her until she struck back, then gave a smile as he backed off.

"Because she wants to make your life better? Jessica doesn't seem like a bad person. Give her a chance." His gray eyes looked into hers before glancing in the rearview mirror to see Jessica pull into a spot behind them.

"Why not? It's not like I can't get any more hurt than I already am." Alyssa opened the door and slid out of the truck, took a deep breath, and plastered a smile on her face.

Jessica herded the teens toward the door. "So, today I thought we could get a new dresser for your room. You have a three-hundred-dollar budget and other than that, it's completely up to you."

Shock and contrition zipped through Alyssa's heart as the wide doors automatically opened, and she found herself in the pristine lobby of a three-story furniture store. Bright colors and clean designs dominated as far as the eye could see, and she took a needed moment to process all of the stimulation.

"I don't understand." Her fingers tucked a stray lock of hair behind her ear as she looked over to where Jessica and Caleb stood in conspiratorial bliss.

Jessica grabbed a cart and gestured toward the entrance to the furniture section. "Well, Bri's mother and I were having lunch the other day, and she mentioned that Brianna was talking about how your dresser wasn't big enough to fit all of the clothes that you need to own, and I thought we would fix that problem. Starting with the dresser, and then Bri can help you with the clothes."

Alyssa felt her ears burn with embarrassment. "No, really, the one I have is just fine. You know Bri, she thinks I need five outfits for each day of the week, even though I'm pretty sure she has just as few clothes as I do."

"Alli." Jessica tried to fix Alyssa with a stern stare, but the smile kept peeking through. "If Bri thinks you need a bigger dresser, then you need a bigger dresser. Besides, I know how little clothes you actually have, and we can definitely afford to add a little to your collection, especially with spring coming up soon. Now come on."

A smile crept onto Alyssa's face as they walked along the aisles of the store, grand displays of bedroom sets surrounding them. A beautiful ceiling fan caught her eye, the delicate green vine pattern with purple flowers standing out against the creamy-white blades. The glass light fixture was a group of tulips, with each petal housing a space for a light bulb, and a tiny glass bumblebee dangled at the end of a pull chain.

"That's pretty," Caleb said from beside her, looking up at the fan.

"Yeah, but we're here to buy a dresser." Alyssa turned away from the fan, shoving the feeling of wanting and disappointment deep into her heart. *Stop wanting more*, she demanded to herself. *Be happy you are getting anything at all.*

Caleb walked to the wall that held the boxes of products and picked up the long box with the fan product tag. "Well, I came here with a couple hundred bucks and no real plans. So, it's going to come home with me. Although ..." He rubbed his chin dramatically, fingers scratching on the stubble that had formed from his teenage rebellion against the razor. "It would look awfully silly in my room, so we had better just be store it in your room, on the ceiling perhaps, instead of in a corner where it might get in the way."

Alyssa turned, mouth hanging slightly open as Jessica just quietly chuckled from her position behind the cart. "Caleb, you don't have to do that."

"No, I don't, but I want to - ooph!" His sentence was cut off as Alyssa flung herself onto him, wrapping her arms around his neck in a rare show of affection.

"Thank you." She disengaged and grinned, practically bouncing as they moved toward a different bedroom display.

After positioning the cart out of foot traffic, Jessica stepped up to a dresser that matched the fan, a cream piece of furniture that stood hip-high, with thin vines and tendrils that formed a border around each of the six drawers. Painted blossoms drifted down the sides of the dresser, and blooms formed the center of each metal drawer handle.

"How about this one, Alyssa? It would match the fan." Jessica pulled open a drawer, happy with the metal hardware and deep storage it provided.

"It's beautiful." Running a hand over the detailed wood, Alyssa knew she could easily fit her clothes in just two of the drawers. Her finger touched the price tag, and her face fell. "It's far too much though. It's fifty dollars over the budget."

Jessica checked the price tag and tapped her finger against her chin. "Well, I did miss the opportunity to get you a Christmas present this year, so how about we just call the extra your Christmas present?"

"But you already got me a Christmas present, remember? The books, I mean. It's okay, really. We'll just find one within the budget." Alyssa took a deep breath and turned away from the dresser to find Jessica with an exasperated look on her face.

"Okay, then it will just be one of your Christmas presents for next year, and it will just be an early present. It's coming home with us, end of negotiation."

"Really?" Alyssa felt a strange lump in her throat at the thought of compromise, or that someone was willing to negotiate so that she could have something she wanted, when she never asked for the dresser in the first place.

"Really. Let's go pick up the pieces." Jessica whistled a happy tune under her breath as the trio made their way to a large section of the store that held the individual parts of the larger furniture.

Wide eyes took in the myriad of boxes as Alyssa looked around in confusion. "But, if it comes in pieces ... I mean, Bri and I did the bookcase, but that was like ... four boards ..."

A grin lit up Caleb's face. "That's the fun part!"

~ * ~ * ~

She was covered in Styrofoam bits, her back hurt from bending over, and her thumb still throbbed from its connection with the hammer, but Alyssa had never felt happier as she climbed into bed that night. The three had worked together as they built the heavy, complicated dresser, Jessica reading the directions as Caleb and Alyssa connected the pieces.

Halfway through the adventure, Brianna stopped by to say hi, then stayed to give moral support and laugh with Jessica over the funny symbols on the instructions. She had no intention of picking up a tool, citing that she had done her job with the bookcase, but frequently brought them glasses of water and told funny jokes when construction grew frustrating and Alyssa was ready to scream.

I built that, Alyssa thought as she laid her head upon her soft pillow and stared at the dresser. It had been an exciting, frustrating, and rewarding experience. From utter panic at the sight of all of the pieces to a calm confidence as they screwed on the last handle, the dresser was something created out of her own intelligence and hard work.

As she closed her eyes and drifted to sleep, she thought, *I may not be good at math, but I sure can build a mean dresser.*

Fourteen

Nervous energy filled the room as Alyssa's English class sat quietly, most tapping their feet on the floor or pencils on the desk. They had just finished their poetry unit and today was the day when they would be required to read one of their poems in front of the class.

Alyssa's leg bounced under the desk, and she silently counted from one to ten and back down again as she tried to find a semblance of calmness. Public speaking was terrifying, knowing that all eyes are upon you, that some students were just waiting for you to make a mistake that they could use against you for the rest of the year.

Her eyes shifted around the room, and caught a small smile of encouragement from Brianna. *At least it seems that everyone else is scared too*, she realized.

Mrs. Callen smiled as she perched on the edge of her desk. "Alrighty, who wants to go first?"

Silence answered her as twenty students looked at their desks, their feet, out the window, anywhere but at the teacher.

"Okay then, we'll go alphabetically." She picked up her roster to make sure she didn't go out of order, something Alyssa knew would be pointed out by some of the students in the class.

"Bailen, Aaron. Let's hear it."

He walked to the front of the class with a swagger, holding a crumpled piece of paper in one hand and waving to the other students with the other. With a dramatic throat clearing and paper rustling, he read, "I have to write a poem, but poetry is dumb. I would rather clean my bedroom, even though that it not fun. I really want to play video games, and I bet so would you, but I have to write a poem, so this piece of crap will do."

Laughter filled the room as he took a bow and then sauntered back to his seat, but Mrs. Callen just shook her head as she scribbled in her grading book.

"Yes, Aaron, good job with the rhyming. Doe, Alyssa. You're up."

Alyssa sighed as she picked up her paper and stood. Last name or first, she was always near the start of the alphabet, something she detested. Her hands shook as she held the paper in front of her, even more terrified after that reading.

How am I supposed to be serious and read my poem after that? She thought as she quickly and quietly panicked. For several seconds she stared at her paper, debating making up something equally superficial before deciding her integrity with the teacher was more important than her upcoming embarrassment.

It was something she had come up with during the dead of night, when the only lights were the soft glow from her nightlight and the one street light outside of her window. She closed her eyes as she read the words, the hope, the longing, the terror of always being alone and the light always being just out of reach. With the final word, she opened her eyes and let out a long, quiet breath.

A moment of unnerving silence, then one member of the class began to clap, followed by another, and yet another, until the entire room filled with applause. Tears welled in Alyssa's eyes as she released her pent-up breath, smiled, and nodded thank you as she made her way back to her seat.

One by one, the students read their poems in front of the class. Alyssa found herself laughing at some, and growing silent with others. The depth of emotions in the classroom surprised her, and scared her. For once, she felt connected with other people her age, started rethinking the idea that they were nothing like her.

They may not know what it is like to not have a home, or be in the system, she mused to herself, *but everyone feels lost and alone in their own way. We're all a little broken inside.*

"Vollora, Brianna."

Legs shaking, Brianna made her way to the front of the room, pulling her long-sleeved shirt down to the palm of her hands. Her head bowed in a moment of thought, and then she took a deep breath and read her work.

Alyssa clapped, though clapping hardly seemed the right reaction to such a poem. Brianna, with her permanent smile and bubbly personality, had created a poem of haunting beauty and turmoil, as if her soul was on the brink of completely despair, the words perfectly capturing that moment of still terror just before taking the plunge into the deep end of life. It tugged at her in a way that no other work read that day had done, as if it had drilled into the core where she kept her darkest thoughts and shined a light upon them.

She leaned over while the teacher had her back to the room, writing the next assignment on the board. "Bri, that was beautiful."

"Thanks," her friend whispered back, tucking the page into her notebook. "That was so scary! I'm so glad you had a serious one too."

Moments later the bell rang, and students filed into the hallway. Since their next classes were next to one another, she and Brianna walked down the hallway, chattering away over the din of moving bodies.

"Do you know where Caleb is today? I didn't see him before school or in class." Alyssa made a quick stop at her locker to switch books and check her reflection in the mirror. She had started wearing mascara and lip gloss, and smiled at the face that stared back at her. It wasn't the make-up itself, but the freedom of being able to wear it that made her so happy.

Brianna shook her head and leaned against the locker. "No, I didn't hear from him all weekend either, did you?"

"Nope. I hope he's okay." Alyssa waved goodbye as she reached her doorway and stepped in. Tucking her backpack into its reserved space between her ankles, she flipped her notebook open to an empty page and wrote down the objectives from the board.

Oh good, she thought as she scrawled across the page, *today we're learning about bank accounts.*

Personal Finance was her favorite, if hardest, class, and she drank in the information like a water-starved desert flower. It was empowering to know how things like credit cards and loans worked, and she felt like she might stand a chance of managing her money when she would, hopefully, get a job. She had seen firsthand how hard it was for kids like her to make it in the real world, and if she could at least understand how money worked, she would have a fighting chance.

Halfway through class, the door opened and Caleb sauntered in, grinning his usual cocky grin as the teacher just shook his head at the lateness. His left knee was stiff as he walked, and when Alyssa looked up to see the black bruises that peeked out from the collar of his shirt, her mood quickly turned dark. She knew what it meant when bruises covered body parts that were not visible to the public, where people like teachers couldn't see them, people who would report it to protective services.

The rest of the lesson was a blur, as Alyssa's mind focused on every movement Caleb made, from the way he constantly rolled his shoulders, as if the muscles were too tight beneath, to the way his breathing hitched every time he took a deep breath.

When the bell rang and the class filed into the hallway, she pushed him into an empty space next to a janitor's closet. "What happened?" she demanded through clenched teeth.

His eyebrow simply raised in response. "It's nothing. No biggie." Caleb turned to go to lunch but was held fast by Alyssa's hand wrapping around his arm.

"I can see the bruises, Caleb. I can see that it hurts you to breathe. I'm not as naive as you seem to think I am." Anger building on his behalf flashed in her eyes as she stared up at her friend, daring him to lie to her again.

Caleb carefully removed her clenched hand from his arm and sighed. "Alli, I was dumb, okay? I had some pot in my dresser and my mom found it. She told Dad and he was pissed. It's not the first time, and won't be the last. I'll be fine. It's just some bruises that I deserve for crap I refuse to care about." He turned to leave and was halted as Alyssa's hand fisted in his shirt.

"It's not fine," she hissed, "and you don't deserve that. No one does."

A look of futility crossed his face as he gave her a friendly kiss on the forehead. "That's why you are awesome. You see me as more than just hopeless, but, Alli, I'm too far gone to save. It's fine. Focus on yourself and don't worry about me."

Alyssa watched in helplessness as he walked to the gym, limping with every step.

Fifteen

Darkness cloaked Alyssa as she huddled in the closet, fourteen-years-old and terrified of the dark. She wrapped an arm around the quivering, silently sobbing boy tucked in the closet beside her, Drew, the biological son of her latest foster mother.

No light squeezed through the tightly fitted closet doors, the blackness so absolute that she couldn't even see the colors on the thin, fleece blanket that had been carefully draped over the two children by Theresa. Her foster mother, one of the few who she referred to as a mother, had taken precious seconds to make sure the blanket fully covered the children, that not so much as a toe, finger, or hair would give away their position in the cluttered closet.

Alyssa felt pressure against her toe, and took a small comfort in knowing that Theresa had also hastily shoved several large suitcases and plastic bins in front of the children, deepening the deception and solidifying their presence as nothing but more random items in the tight space.

"I scared, Lyssa," the four-year-old next to her whimpered.

"Shhhh," she calmly admonished, and wrapped her arms more tightly around him. Drew's small head dropped to her chest and she felt his tears soaking through her cotton pajama shirt.

Both children jumped as a sharp scream pierced the too-still night, and quick footsteps pounded down the wooden hallway. Muffled voices could be heard through the layers of fleece and closet doors, Theresa's, and a strange male.

Silent tears coursed down Alyssa's face as they huddled in the dark, her chest growing tighter with every breath taken in their dark hole, and she held on to the thin traces of control only for Drew's sake. *Count to ten*, she thought, *now back down to one, now back up to ten, just like Theresa taught you.* Over and over again as a flurry of footsteps sounded through the house, followed by glass breaking and male cursing.

After what seemed like an eternity, sirens reached her ears, and she felt Drew's head raise from her shoulder.

"Safe now?" he whispered.

"Not yet," she replied. "Shh, stay quiet now. I'm here to protect you."

She felt him snuggle in tighter to his side, his clammy hand gripping hers tightly as his breathing began to quicken.

A blast of fresh air hit them as the closet doors were flung open, and both children recoiled as the blanket was pulled from their heads. Alyssa instinctively pushed Drew behind her, crouching down like a mountain lion and snarling at the silhouetted forms in front of her.

"Easy now, easy. Everything is okay now. We are the police, and here to help. Easy now." The man's body came into focus and Alyssa could see the uniform, the badge, and the gun on his hip. The two children crept out of the closet, fingers locked tightly together, and walked to the front door.

Theresa's husband, Nathan, stood in the yard, his face haggard and tense, but his eyes lit up when he saw the children come out of the house. Hands still together, Alyssa and Andrew ran to him, wrapping themselves around his legs as if he were a life-ring.

Then the cop came over, had some quiet words with her foster father, and gently pulled Alyssa away. Drew screamed, "No! No leave me, Lyssa," his small voice ringing over the sirens as they moved her into the black police vehicle and drove away.

~ * ~ * ~

She jerked awake, thrashing in panic at the comforter that had covered her face, terrified that she was once again hiding in the closet. Though she finally clawed away the fabric and felt fresh air upon her face, it was still dark, blindingly dark, and she looked around in panic for the sources of light that were her beacons: the night-light in her room, the street light out her window, the thin line of yellow glow from the bathroom light that Jessica always left on for her.

The room began to close in on her, and Alyssa whimpered in the darkness. She bolted out of bed, brought down abruptly as her foot tangled in her sheets and sent her crashing to the ground. Disoriented from the blindness and from the fear, she curled into a small ball at the foot of her bed, rocking back and forth as she withdrew into herself.

"Alyssa, you okay?" Jessica's sleepy voice came through the door. "Alli? I heard a thump."

The door opened wider, the flashlight in Jessica's hand shining a beam of light around the room. "Oh, sweetheart."

Soft arms wrapped around Alyssa where she sat rocking in the night. She glanced up and took the offered flashlight, crushing it against her chest hard enough to bruise. "What's going on? Where are the lights?"

"Power outage. The company said a tree went down a few roads over and it should be fixed in a few hours. Want to come out in the living room with me and we can set up some candles?"

She nodded numbly, standing with Jessica's help. With the flashlight clutched in a white-knuckle grip in one hand, and Jessica's hand in the other, Alyssa moved down the hallway and to the living room.

"Sit here while I get some candles."

The room grew dark again as Jessica took the flashlight to find the candles and one of her fiancé's lighters. Alyssa curled into a ball on the couch, pressing her body as deep into the corner cushions as it would possible go, and stared at the small light that bounced off kitchen cabinets as Jessica searched.

"Here we go!" Jessica returned and set up four large pillar candles on the table in front of them, lighting them one by one. A warm yellow glow filled the room, and the scent of apple pie and lavender filled the air.

Alyssa felt Jessica's eyes upon her face and curled into a deeper ball.

Jessica gently touched Alyssa's shoulder before speaking. "Alli, honey, you okay? I'm here to listen if you want to talk about it."

Her tear streaked cheeks and wide eyes took away her chance to lie, so Alyssa whispered, "I had a nightmare. I was trapped in the closet again with Drew, and then they took me away."

Legs pulled up on the couch, Jessica took a sharp breath. "How old were you?"

"Fourteen," Alyssa whispered. "He was only four. We were both asleep and some noise woke us all up. My foster mother, Theresa, came into my room and grabbed me, pulling me into his room. Then she pushed both of us into the closet, kissed us and said she loved us, and said we had to hide. It was so dark, and there were so many scary noises, and then finally the cops came to let us out."

She sniffed and scrubbed at the moisture on her cheeks. "The entire time Drew was so scared, and I told him that I would be there to keep him safe. And then when it was over, we ran out to Dad, and he said everything was going to be okay. Someone had broken into the house and Mom had gotten hurt, but he said she would be okay, and everything was going to be okay because he would just take care of us until she got better."

"But then the police officer pulled me away, and he put me in the cop car. Drew kept screaming for me to come back. I can still hear him screaming when it's quiet. Everything was going to be okay, but they took me away and didn't let me go back. One said that it was too traumatic for me, that it would be too damaging for me to go back to that house, like being pulled away from them wasn't horrible. The other said that Theresa's injuries were too severe, and since they didn't know when she'd be out of the hospital, it was easier to put me in respite care until the details were hashed out. But then I just went into another home, and another, and they never sent me back and I never found out why."

Jessica simply opened her arms and wrapped them tightly around Alyssa's shoulders when the teen collapsed into her lap. "That would have been so scary, and you were so strong and brave to have kept quiet and been there for Drew. Sometimes the rules don't seem to make sense, and sometimes they just plain suck, but the officers still had to follow them."

"I know, but I didn't even get to say goodbye to Drew." Alyssa's head dropped onto Jessica's shoulder on its own accord, and her body curled up against the woman's side. "I abandoned him, even though it wasn't my choice. What if he grows up to be just as mental as me?"

"Oh, Alli. You are not mental." Gentle fingers stroked Alyssa's hair, lulling away the fear and regret. "You are a young woman who has been through more in sixteen years than most people go through in their lifetime, but you are strong, and smart, and resourceful, and you're going to make it to the top in the end, because you are stubborn enough to not accept anything but the best and determined enough to make it happen."

A small chuckle vibrated Alyssa's chest. "I definitely never thought of myself as any of those things." Her dark eyes looked up at Jessica's, and her teeth worried at her lip as she gathered courage to ask, "Do you think we could look up the family? Maybe just send them an email, to let Drew know that I didn't mean to leave him?"

"I'll see what I can do." The woman and the girl curled up together on the couch, brainstorming the email between sleepy yawns, until, leaning against one another, they drifted back to sleep.

Sixteen

Humming happily to herself, Alyssa practically skipped down the school hallway to Brianna's locker. Yesterday, Jessica had taken her to get her hair cut and styled, and the layers bounced and brushed against her cheeks and shoulders as she moved.

I get the big deal about haircuts now! She thought as she ran her fingers through her hair. No former keeper had let her cut her hair, besides trimming split ends, for fear of reprimand from the system. It had been a constant source of strife for her, begging her keepers to cut it shorter, especially after she hit puberty and the boys made jokes about long hair being useful in the sack.

She never really understood the comments, but the way they looked when they said them made Alyssa's stomach churn. She just wanted it shorter so that showers wouldn't take so long, and she wouldn't have to worry about remembering to braid it every night, or dealing a mess of tangles in the morning.

Now, it cascaded in layers, resting just above her shoulders, her head and her mood feeling ten times lighter as she bounced down the hallway.

"Bri!" she called out down the hallway. "What do you think of my hair? Isn't it cute?"

As her friend turned, Alyssa saw the blank expression on Brianna's face the split- second before a smile replaced it. "Yeah, it's totally cute."

"Hey, you okay?" She slung an arm around Bri's shoulder. While her skin still rolled when other people touched it, she was getting better with showing affection, and knew that Brianna was a touchy-feely kind of friend.

Today, Brianna just shrugged off her arm and turned to look back into her locker. "Yep."

Mind spinning, Alyssa popped over to Brianna's other side. "So, Jessica gave me fifty bucks and is driving me to the mall after school to buy some new clothes for spring. Want to come with us?"

"No thanks," her friend answered quietly, still staring into the immaculately organized locker.

Alyssa raised an eyebrow and put her hand on Brianna's shoulder. "Okay, now I know something is wrong. You never turn down shopping."

Brianna slammed her locker shut, quietly growling, "I'm fine, Alli. Nothing is wrong."

Annoyance simmered in Alyssa's chest as she stared at Brianna, knowing that she was lying and not able to understand why her best friend would keep denying that something was obviously wrong. For a second, she had doubts about their friendship, felt the old demons creeping in, saying that she was getting too close and was unwanted, before Brianna looked away from the locker and she could see into her shimmering blue eyes.

That look was familiar; she had seen it at thirteen when she was swimming in the backyard pool of a neighbor. They had thrown a Fourth of July barbeque and invited Alyssa's foster family over, and she had been thrilled to be included. Laughter, water fights, hamburgers, and sparklers had filled their day with joy.

Then the foster parents' three-year-old boy had fallen into the pool, several feet away from Alyssa. One minute he was happily playing with his cars on one of the lawn chairs, and the next he was plunging headfirst into the cold water. He must have been trying to retrieve one of his cars that had rolled to the edge of the pool, and lost his balance as he bent over to pick it up.

She had been the closest one to him, and with a few powerful strokes she was able to wrap her arms around his chest and pull him above the water, helping him out of the pool before the shocked parents were able to cross the fifteen feet between the patio and the water.

Brianna had the same look in her eyes as that little boy. Fear, desperation, hopelessness, acceptance of the inevitable. While she may not have been anywhere near water, Alyssa knew that her friend was drowning. Arms wrapping about Brianna's shoulders, she pitched her voice low for privacy.

"No, you're not fine. But we're going to get you there. Together. Okay?"

Tears welling in her eyes, Brianna nodded, and they both heard the bell ring for class. She sniffed and put on a brave smile. "Talk about it after school, okay?"

"I'll be here whenever you are ready."

~ * ~ * ~

The rubber swing creaked as she swung, cold twilight air rushing against Alyssa's face as she gave Brianna time to find the words to describe her feelings. A creak sounded from the swing beside her, and she heard Brianna take a deep breath.

"I don't know what to do, Alli."

"About what?" Alyssa glanced at her, noticing that her friend had dug a small hole in the dirt under the swing, and now sat with her cheek pressed against the chilled metal.

She shrugged, the herringbone pattern of her thick wool coat rising and falling with the motion. "Everything. School. Friends. Life. It's just so damn hard, and I don't know why. Sometimes just breathing is such a struggle."

Alyssa remained silent a moment, pushing her swing back and forth with her feet, trying to find the right words to help.

Brianna wiped away a tear and leaned back in the swing. "You know what, it's stupid. Just pretend I didn't say anything. Everything is fine. I shouldn't have dragged you into this mess and just kept on letting you see the happy side of me."

"Hey." Alyssa gently pulled on the chain of Brianna's swing to bring her closer. "If it has you this upset, then it's not stupid. Definitely not nothing, which means it's something. And you are totally not fine right now and I'm glad you are letting me in."

"I have no right, none at all, to talk to you about life being difficult." She gave a bitter laugh that turned into a sob and swatted at another tear that dropped from her eye. "That's what makes it harder though. I have absolutely nothing to complain about, and yet ..."

"Bri," Alyssa began.

"No!" she interrupted. "I know it's true. I have two loving parents in a committed marriage, and a big house, and pets, and a room filled with clothes, and pretty much anything I ever wanted, within reason. I've never had to worry about having food to eat, or clothes to wear, or boys touching me without permission. It's not like I'm rich and going to be driving a Benz or anything, but I know that when I get my license I'll have a car to drive and parents who will let me drive it and be able to call it my own."

Brianna paused, and Alyssa could see the metal chain shaking from the trembling of her friend's body. She reached out and held out her hand, palm up, in the air next to her. Brianna reached out and took it, linking her fingers with Alyssa and holding tight, as if it were a rope ready to pull her to shore.

"It's just, I'm so sad, all the time. Every night I cry myself to sleep. Every morning it's a struggle just to get out of bed, just to find motivation to leave the house. Most days I second guess everything, friendships, my future, that my parents really love me. And I can't tell anyone because no one would understand why I feel this way, because even I don't, and they would just tell me to grow up and get a thicker skin and deal with it. It's just so stupid. Most days I just want to curl up into a hole somewhere and never come out, just so I don't have to deal with it anymore."

Her face was red and puffy, eyes black-ringed from smudged mascara and cheeks glimmering as the rays of the setting sun reflected off her tears. When she looked at Alyssa, Brianna's eyes were filled with misery and guilt. "I don't have any right to feel this way, and I know that. Not when so many bad things have happened to other people. I know that, and it just makes it harder. Life shouldn't be this damn hard. I've spent so many years faking happiness, pretending to be the perky girl everyone loves, but I just can't do it anymore. I can't keep holding together when I know I'm falling apart."

Jumping off the swing, Alyssa caught Brianna as her body slumped forward into a sobbing heap, and the two girls sat, arms wrapped tightly around one another, in the cold mud below the swings.

"Bri," Alyssa began, holding her friend close and gently stroking her hair. "You have every right to feel this way. So what if your life seems perfect to everyone else, that doesn't mean you don't have feelings. That doesn't mean that you can't feel sad, or overwhelmed, or lost. Just because you haven't had something tragic happen to you doesn't mean that you have to be happy and perfect all the time."

For several minutes, Brianna just cried harder, chest shaking and nose running, and Alyssa knew that she had never let anyone else see even a glimpse of the misery and darkness within. Of anyone, she had first-hand experience with putting up the mask of perfection, the happy little girl without a mean thought in the world. She hugged Brianna tighter, feeling something within her click into place as she realized she could be a light in the darkness for her friend, an anchor in the storm known as Hurricane Brianna.

When the sobbing subsided, Alyssa gave the other girl a soft poke in the shoulder. "I think you need to tell someone how you feel." She held up a hand as Brianna went to interrupt, panic filling her eyes. "Maybe not your parents, because I know that would be a huge step, but maybe talk to a counselor at school or call one of those anonymous hotlines or something."

"They'll just say I'm being dramatic," she whispered, vocal cords raw and sore from crying. "It won't make any difference. I don't think I would even believe how miserable I am. What if they sent me away to a hospital?"

"No they won't, and yes, it will, and no they won't." Alyssa stood up and tugged Brianna to her feet. "I won't let them send you anywhere you don't want to go. You've been my rock, now let me be yours."

Brianna linked her pinky with Alyssa's as a promise, then flung her arms around her. "I love you, Alyssa. Thank you for being my best friend."

"I love you too," Alyssa replied, not even a little terrified of the feeling.

Seventeen

The smell of pancakes wafted through the air as Alyssa slowly opened her eyes and stretched. *I slept until noon again*? She thought in amazement. It was still new to her that she could sleep in as long as she wanted on the weekend, and she felt a twinge of guilt that every Saturday she was awoken to the smell of pancakes and bacon, without her having to lift a finger.

As she pulled out a pair of jeans and a long-sleeved shirt from her dresser, she lovingly ran a finger over the delicate designs and painted vines. She still couldn't believe her good luck at being able to own such a beautiful piece of furniture.

Enjoy it while you can, that little bleak voice whispered, and Alyssa pushed it back as she pulled her hair into a loose braid.

Jessica was already sitting at the table when she walked out, and gestured to the large stack of pancakes. "Help yourself, kiddo. Up late last night?"

"Yeah," Alyssa reluctantly admitted as she put two pancakes onto a porcelain plate and poured the syrup. "We have a test on banking tomorrow, like interest and investing decisions and stuff like that, and I just can't figure it out to save my life."

"Mmm," Jessica mumbled through a mouthful of pancake. "I'd imagine it would be hard for most kids your age to get it, when you haven't actually had the experience of managing large sums of money. If you want, you and I can go over it tonight after dinner. I'd be glad to try to explain it in a different way than the book, or we can use game money to practice the different concepts to give you a visual."

Alyssa perked up in her chair and felt relief flush through her. "That would be awesome, Jessica. Thank you so much." Her finance class had been one of the hardest so far, and she had put extra pressure on herself to get good grades, and really know the material inside and out, instead of just memorizing the facts. She needed it to survive in the future and she knew it.

No, thrive in the future, she chastised herself. *I will not merely survive, not anymore. Now I will fly and make the future wonderful, whatever I want it to be.*

That was one thing that Jessica had done, Alyssa had realized last night as she lay in bed staring at the glow-in-the-dark stars that she had placed on her ceiling in exact constellations. While part of her mind and heart still sat waiting for the blow, anticipating the inevitable bad news or hammer to fall, she had hope now.

And not naïve hope, she mused as she finished her pancakes and took her plate to the sink. *Real hope.*

Then a thought dawned on her, and she frowned slightly as she rinsed the plate. "But, Jess, isn't tonight your date night with Darren?"

Jessica's chest rose and fell before she answered, and Alyssa could hear the tightness in her keeper's voice that usually was in her own. "We rescheduled. Something came up, so my night is free for a girl's night. Plus," she stood up and brought her own dish to the sink, giving Alyssa and affectionate hip bump. "I have a feeling we'll be a little preoccupied tonight with the surprise I have for you, and with doing some homework."

"A surprise? For me? What is it?" Alyssa twirled the end of her braid around her finger. Surprises always made her nervous, the excitement quickly overridden by fear. The first boy she had ever friended after she went into the system was big on surprises, the first kid she met with an attitude. At first the surprises were benign, a flower, a necklace, maybe a dead beetle, which, while creepy, actually was quite beautiful depending on the species.

Then his surprises turned darker, and when they became drugs, she cut off the friendship without looking back, which was not something he was happy about. She bore the black-eye for a week while telling others she had walked into a door, clumsy her, in order to avoid any further confrontation.

"If I told you, it wouldn't be a surprise, now would it?" Jessica winked, then her voice softened. "It's a good thing, hon. Go grab your backpack."

She did, double checking that her phone, wallet, and keys were safely stashed inside the outer pocket. It meant a lot to her that Jess understood how important the backpack was to her, and didn't push for her to leave it behind or try to replace it. Slowly,

Alyssa was starting to feel more comfortable with the idea of returning to the house every time she left, but still not enough to take a chance at losing her most valued possession.

Her cell phone was always within quick reach, even if she was just taking a shower or sitting on the front porch. At least with that, she would never have to feel separated again, never feel alone and lost, as long as she had some connection to Brianna and Caleb.

As if on cue, her phone buzzed in her purse. She pulled it out and snickered at the hilarious picture of Caleb, dressed in a bright blue princess gown and with a plastic tiara on his head, courtesy of his play-date with his little sister.

Looking up, she saw a hint of a smile on Jessica's face, as if she were trying to hide it away. "Caleb again?"

"Yeah, he's baby-sitting his sister and showed me what they've been up to this morning. He looks good in a ball gown." Alyssa giggled again as she showed the picture to Jessica, who laughed as she shook her head.

"Do you and I need to have the big talk then?" She winked to lighten the question. "You seem to like him a lot."

Alyssa shoved her phone in her backpack and looked at Jessica in disbelief. "Oh my god, no. We're just friends. I totally don't look at him that way. Besides …"

"Besides?"

"I don't exactly have a good history of romance. Role models, I mean. It's far better to keep someone as a friend forever, than risk losing them because you fall out of love, you know?"

Jessica locked the door and walked out to the car before answering. "Everyone needs a little love though. Don't you think it's better to love and have your heart broken than never love at all?"

A harsh laugh escaped Alyssa as she settled in the car, and she looked away apologetically. "Sorry, it's just, I've had my heart broken by adults so many times already, I don't know if I could survive having it broken by someone my age."

"Just let me know if you're ready, okay? I don't want you to get into trouble if your heart falls faster than your head can keep up." She glanced over at Alyssa, then pulled out of the driveway and headed downtown.

Alyssa gave a nervous giggle, as she rested her head against the seat,. "Oh, believe me, even if my heart falls my body won't be following. That's how my mom screwed up her life, by having me, and I have absolutely no intent on going down that path or forcing another child to grow up like this."

Jessica's body jerked slightly, and she tapped her fingers nervously on the steering wheel. "Are you ready to talk about your mom?"

Alyssa shrugged. "What do you want to know? I would think it was in my file or something."

"Some of it, in a very clinical sense. What do you remember about her?"

Closing her eyes, she tried to remember her life before that day at school, a life when she felt she had a family, even if it was a dysfunctional one. "At first, she was just like every other mom, I guess. She would play with me, dolls or trains, or just run around in the yard, at least, she would try. Then, it was like she just gave up. She would just scream at everything, even inanimate objects like the stove because it wasn't heating dinner fast enough."

"And nothing I did was right, or good enough, ever. I could never be clean enough, or cute enough, or just … anything enough for her. When I think back, all I can remember is that she smelled like alcohol, even though I never saw any drinks in her hand, and she was always mad or crying.

"Sometimes," her breath caught as the words came out in a whisper, "sometimes I think I must have done something horrible to make Daddy leave. If I had just been a better baby, maybe he would have stayed, and Mom wouldn't have been so angry and sad all the time, and we could have all just been happy."

Jessica reached over and squeezed Alyssa's hand hard, taking the other off the wheel momentarily to wipe at her eyes. "There is nothing you did to cause their marriage to fall apart, and nothing you could have done to keep them together. I know it's hard to believe that, but it's true. Their marriage might have been destined to fail from the start, and if it wasn't you, it would have been any other kid." Another squeeze. "You are wonderful, Alyssa Doe. And don't you ever let anyone tell you otherwise."

Eighteen

"Bri! You have got to come over right away! Like, right now, this second, right away. Jessica gave me the best surprise yesterday." Alyssa forced herself to lower her voice level as it rose in her excitement. The sound of Jessica chuckling from the other room filtered through the half-closed door and a blush crept up Alyssa's cheeks.

Ten minutes later, Bri was bouncing into her bedroom, and her arrival was stopped short as she shrieked in excitement. "Oh-em-gee, that is the cutest freaking thing I've ever seen!"

The orange kitten stared at both girls with an expression of excitement and terror before becoming distracted by a glittery ball and pouncing.

Alyssa grabbed one of the cat toys that she and Jessica had purchased at the pet store and slowly dragged it across her bed, laughing as the tiny kitten got tangled in her own tail and did a floppy somersault. "Jessica said it was getting far too boring in here, so we added this little munchkin to our family. Isn't she perfect? We named her Tulip and I love her already."

"She is pretty dang adorable, I didn't realize females could be orange too! I thought it was just the males. You got a special one!" Brianna gushed as the kitten jumped into her lap and started kneading her jeans. "That's so cool of Jessica to get you a cat!"

"Yeah, she's pretty awesome," Alyssa admitted as she sat cross-legged on the bed. She looked at Brianna and noted the dark circles under her eyes. "Still can't sleep?"

A shrug was the answer, and Brianna focused all of her attention on the cat.

Alyssa scooted closer so their knees touched. "How did your therapy session go?"

Tears welled up in Brianna's eyes. "He thinks that I need medication. He said there is probably something off in my brain that is making me have such fatalistic thoughts, and making me sad all the time. But medicine is for sick people. I don't want to be sick, or dependent on chemicals to make me happy."

"It's not your fault, you know," Alyssa said gently. "You can't help your body chemistry, or how you feel. You just feel it. I think you should give it a shot and see what happens. I mean, he's going to give you other stuff to do too, right?"

She sniffed and scratched Tulip under her tiny chin. "Yeah. I have different breathing exercises and thought processes and stuff to try to help too."

"So, maybe the medicine will just help you feel a little more stable, a little stronger, and then you'll be able to just go with those exercises. It will be like someone with diabetes having to take insulin, or someone who can't walk using a wheelchair."

Brianna shrugged in response, so Alyssa asked the question she feared most.

"How are your parents taking this?"

A tear rolled down Brianna's cheek and fell onto the tabby furball in her lap. "My mom cried a lot, and my dad is still really confused. They don't understand how this could happen to me, and keep blaming themselves, even though I told them that it's nothing they did, or could prevent. They keep treating me like I'm fragile, like if they yell at me, I'll go jump off a cliff or something."

"Will you?"

"I'm not that depressed," Brianna's voice held a note of the sass that Alyssa loved so well. She huffed out a breath and gave a small chuckle. "I think of all of these bad things, but I don't have any desire to do it, you know? I mean, I get where they are coming from. They said they will always stand beside me and support me, even though they don't know what to do to help me. I don't even know what to do with me, so I can't imagine that they would know what to do with me. Okay, that made no sense. I'm just going to stop talking."

A snort escaped as Alyssa playfully gave her best friend a shoulder bump, "Bri, I love you, but you never make sense, and that's never stopped you from talking before."

"I swear, it's like you and Caleb share a freaking mind. He just told me the same thing the other day. You two had better not fall in love or anything, because then the world would just like, implode or something."

"Seriously? You too? Jess was on my butt about him the other day. He is totally not my type." Alyssa lay back on her pillow, then gave a muffled scream as Tulip made a mad jump attack for her earrings.

"It would be an awesome story though. The dark, dangerous man with a mohawk who is on every teacher's black list, falls in love with the good girl who is always well-mannered. And then you'd have little babies who were all perfectly behaved, but wore studded necklaces and crap."

"You are twisted," Alyssa replied, although she couldn't stop the laughter that bubbled out with the mental image of her and Caleb as a couple. "First off, no. Besides, he's more like a brother to me than any kind of romantic interest."

"Alright then, what is your type?"

Alyssa paused a moment in her tickling of the cat to think. "Tall, clean cut, a guy who is going to take care of his family no matter what happens. Someone who is just interesting enough to hold attention, but not so 'out there' as to always attract attention." She shook her head and rolled her eyes. "Not like I'll ever find someone like that, not with my past, and not before I'm like, fifty. Besides, no guy is going to want someone who doesn't want to be touched, and who has no interest in sex."

"No interest in ... Are you even human? I've never had it, but that doesn't mean I'm not interested." Brianna dropped her voice lower as the girls heard Jessica's barely concealed snort of laughter from the living room.

"It's not that big of a deal. I mean, I never wanted to do it, even before ... Never mind. Forget I even brought up the subject. Look, a shiny object!" Alyssa pointed to a blank spot on the wall before she drew her knees to her chest and hugged them tightly, fighting the memories.

She could tell Brianna noticed, and her friend lightly tapped her toe against Alyssa's socked foot. "Hey, we're like sisters now. You can tell me anything and it will only make me love you more."

Tears slid out of Alyssa's eyes before she could blink them back, but she shook her head vehemently. "Not yet. I don't think I can talk about it to anyone yet."

"Well," Brianna said lovingly, "when you are ready, I'm here. Always."

Nineteen

A groan escaped Caleb's lips as Alyssa chuckled behind her copy of *Walk the Red Road*. The coffee shop around them had been packed when they arrived, and they were lucky to grab a small table in the back corner. Now it was empty, and Caleb had been whining about the stupidity of English essays for the past five minutes.

"Tell me again why I'm writing this paper and not just blowing it off like all of my other ones?" His eyebrows lifted as his gray eyes gave Alyssa a woeful look.

"Because if you fail English, I will be so pissed at you that I will never talk to you again, and then I'd be doubly upset at you, which will make you more upset, so doing the paper is just easier for both of us." She gave him a glare to emphasize the point, then dissolved into giggles as he picked up his pen, grumbling about stubborn females who did not appreciate the fine art of procrastination.

"I do too know a lost cause when I see one," she responded after a few minutes of listening to his grumbles. "I am one, remember?"

Caleb shook his head and pointed at her with his pen. "*You* are not a lost cause. You are a hawk who has had her wings clipped for so long that she has forgotten to fly. But when they fully heal and you are let out of the cage, you are going to soar, Alyssa, so high above everyone else that we will just be dots below, forever forgotten."

"While I have every intention of flying, I will never forget you," she replied, and then her eyes narrowed as she saw Jessica walk through the door with an older couple. "Who do you think that is?"

"Um, Jessica? Your aunt? The lady you live with?"

"No, the couple she's with. Stop being so annoying."

"Huh, don't know," Caleb responded. "I've never seen them here before."

Jessica hovered at the door as the older couple approached the counter and ordered their coffee. Instinct had Alyssa tucking her nose into her book, not knowing who they were, but not feeling comfortable that they could see over the divided wall.

Alyssa peeked over the book and caught Caleb's look of irritation as the couple sat at the table on the other side of the wall, their voices drifting over the wooden barrier but out of view.

"Look, Jessica. I understand where you are coming from, but you have to think of your future," the male voice sounded irritated. "You are a young woman with the rest of your life ahead of you -"

Jessica's voice interrupted, her voice pitched as it often was when she spoke to Darren while upset and her words became clipped. "Yes, Dad, I know. And nothing about the rest of my life has changed, at least as far as I am concerned."

"Darling," the female began to speak, her voice like sticky honey coating Alyssa's ears, "it's just that Darren is afraid that you are throwing your life away for charity, and I'm afraid we agree with him."

"Charity?" Jessica gave a bark of laughter and Alyssa could picture her throwing her head back in disbelief. "Charity has nothing to do with it. Try love, or duty, fixing a wrong, or actually having a heart, unlike some people I know."

The man spoke again, his tone one that would be used to placate an unreasonable child. "Jessica, honey, you aren't thinking about this rationally. What about your own children, what about your wedding? How are you and Darren going to accomplish all of your dreams if you have a teenager tagging along? Her mother threw away her life by refusing to end the pregnancy at the start, don't throw away your own by taking her in."

Alyssa realized they were speaking about her and felt as if she had fallen into frigid water, her chest slowly being crushed by the pressure. For a terrifying moment, she couldn't remember how to breathe, and her vision blurred so much she felt dizzy. Then there was warmth on her hand, and she wrapped her fingers around the anchor known as Caleb, and simply returned his stare as her breathing returned to normal.

He placed a finger across his lips, keeping his hold on her hand, grounding her as they continued to eavesdrop.

Now, she could tell, they had truly rattled Jessica's cages. "Her mother was a teenage drama queen who never felt good enough for you, never good enough for anyone, so she rolled over for any boy who said he loved her. Don't you dare compare me to her, not any more, not ever."

"And you think the girl is going to be any different?" the female voice dripped with disbelief. "The girl has probably already slept with more boys than she can remember, and who knows what kind of drugs she discovered while going through the system. I'm begging you, Jess, don't throw away your life because you feel like you need to fix her."

"She has not done any of that. And how dare you think that Alyssa will end up the same way, when she has already beaten so many odds to be where she is today." Jessica's voice was quiet now, frightfully controlled, and Alyssa cringed behind the wall as silent tears poured from her eyes.

Jessica continued, "Alyssa is an incredible young woman, who has only grown stronger through her struggles. If you had taken any initiative at all to be in her life, you would have known that, but instead you chose to pretend she never existed in the first place." A chair scraped and Alyssa stared at the reflection of Jessica in her water glass.

"But her mother ..."

"Yes, her mother screwed up," Jessica agreed. "She was a spoiled little brat and a slut and married young and everything else you guys told me. She threw away Alyssa and screwed up by having a kid as a teenager, I will agree with you on that. But Alyssa deserves her second chance, and there is nothing you can say or do that will cause me to take that away from her."

Alyssa continued to watch as Jessica stormed out of the coffee shop, followed by the older couple. She felt as if a razor blade had been scraped against her heart, and all of the hope sucked from her body.

This couple didn't even know her, but they had stated every fear she had about Jessica, every doubt about Jessica keeping her for any length of time. Their words smashed through the fragile garden of hope and love that she had been so carefully cultivating and left her feeling shattered and alone.

"Alli, look at me." Caleb's deep voice held no hesitation, no questioning, so she looked. "You are loved, and it's going to take more than two nuts to convince Jessica to give up on you. I don't know who they were, but I do know you, and I know Jessica, and you two belong together. Hold onto her, and me, and Bri. Opposition be damned, we're not letting you be abandoned ever again."

Twenty

The repetitive motion of gliding the brush over Thunder's back was soothing, helping to ease away the emotional aches and pains of the last week. As the bristles gently dislodged dust and hay from the bay Thoroughbred's thin coat, Alyssa felt as if her own debris was being washed away, another layer of hope coming through.

"You know, for being a former racehorse, you're pretty darn lazy," she joked as she gave the gelding an affectionate scratch.

It was only her third time as a volunteer at Bayberry, but Wendy had assigned her the tall horse as her special project. While Alyssa did feel a small pang of hurt at not being given the chance to work with the lost horse, Yuda, she immediately fell in love with Thunder.

Giving his shoulder a nudge so he would move away from the wall and she could move to his other side, she giggled and said, "You definitely took advantage of your second chance, didn't you, boy?"

Thunder snorted in reply, spraying water and saliva around the stall, barely missing Alyssa as she ducked out of the way.

"Oh, that is so disgusting. How can you be so beautiful and so gross at the same time?" She shook her head as she started brushing down his other side.

He definitely got lucky, she thought as she once again fell into a trance. A racehorse who didn't have the heart to win, Wendy found Thunder at a horse auction in Kentucky. There to look at potential candidates for her brand-new therapy center, she had immediately passed over the dark bay, knowing a racehorse would never be calm enough for what her clients needed.

But when Wendy walked by his stall the second time, on her way back out to the entrance, he stuck out his head and stopped her dead in her tracks. When the auction went underway, no one wanted him, except for one horse trainer who she knew had a bad reputation, so she threw in a low bid.

Alyssa still remembered Wendy chuckling as she told the story. She had purchased the horse for two hundred dollars, dirt cheap compared to the thousands and tens of thousands the other animals were going for during that day.

The gelding shifted, and Alyssa sucked in her breath as he pressed her against the stall. "You big galumph, move over!" She gently poked his ribs with her finger and took a deep breath as he shifted away. He turned his head to look back at her, and she couldn't help but laugh at the twinkle in his eye. "You totally did that on purpose."

"It's because he likes you," Wendy's voice came from the other side of the tall horse's body.

"He tries to kill me because he likes me?" Alyssa asked, carefully ducking under his neck to hang up the water bucket Wendy had placed in front of the stall door.

"What can I say?" Wendy shrugged. "He's a boy. Boys do weird things when they like you."

Alyssa clipped the water bucket, arms shaking under the weight, and then dusted her hands off on her jeans. "I'll take your word for it. I don't want anything to do with boys, human ones, that is."

For a long moment, Wendy just stared at her, then spoke just as Alyssa was starting to feel uncomfortable with the silence. "You want to take a ride?"

"What?" Alyssa choked out.

"You know, up there," Wendy gestured to Thunder's back, chuckling as she did.

"I don't know how." Voice growing tight with fear of the unknown, Alyssa began to back away from the horse.

"Then I will teach you," was the calm response, as Wendy carried in a saddle pad, saddle, and bridle. "Here is how we get him ready. First, put the saddle pad on like so, and then the saddle. Then we want to tighten up the girth."

Alyssa laughed as Thunder took a big breath, filling his lungs with air and expanding his chest. Wendy just waited patiently, a small smile on her face, then smoothly tightened the belt-looking piece of leather when it was finally released.

"Now this is the bridle, this is what you use to help give him direction. First you take off the halter, then put this on." Wendy smoothly removed the nylon halter and slid the leather bridle in place.

"Isn't there supposed to be something in his mouth?"

Wendy gave the large horse a pat before leading him into the aisle. "Typically, yes. But we found out this old boy does so much better without one, that we've started riding him that way. I'm going to connect you to a lead-line anyway, so you won't have to worry about what your hands are doing quite so much while you are focusing on staying on his back."

They stepped into the large ring, and Alyssa smiled at the short, leather boots placed next to the large block of wood used for getting onto the horses. At Wendy's insistence, she put them on, tucking her tennis shoes out of the way.

Thunder stopped in front of the block and Wendy walked to where Alyssa stood. "Now, put your foot in the stirrup here, and you are just going to swing your right leg up and over his back."

Alyssa did, taking a moment to breathe as she realized how tall Thunder really was, and that the sandy floor seemed really far below.

"Ready?"

She nodded, squeezing both of the reins in one tight fist and clenching the horse's rough mane in the other. He moved forward, and she felt her body move with the motion, hips slowly swaying side to side as she gradually relaxed on his back.

"There you go. Relax. He knows what to do. He may be a little much for our clients, but he'll take good care of you."

Puffing out a breath, Alyssa felt a smile grow on her face as they completed the first lap around the sandy ring. By the third, her cheeks hurt from grinning and she had relaxed enough for Wendy to show her the proper way to hold the reins.

"I think you are a natural at this. We'll have to start working rides in more often, since it will be good for both of you. He doesn't get nearly the amount of exercise he deserves, so it would be doing me a huge favor. What do you think? You game?"

"Yes!" Alyssa all but shouted, then blushed at her enthusiasm.

"Good deal then." Wendy looked at her watch and then back at the office. "Ah crap, I totally forgot about my meeting with the school reps. If I untack him, do you think you could give him another quick brushing?"

"Oh, totally." Legs aching slightly from the light exercise, Alyssa slid off the gelding ungracefully, grateful for the steadying hand as Wendy caught her.

Ten minutes later, Thunder was untacked and rebrushed, and Alyssa headed toward the parking lot to wait for Jessica.

Jessica was already there, and stood with her back to Alyssa, elbows on the car with the phone pressed to her ear. "Yes, Patricia, I understand the point but ... No, I don't. I think it would be really helpful to Alyssa if I could just tell her that we're ... I get that ... It would help her realize this is a permanent solution if she knew ... Alright, alright. I hear you. I'll wait a little longer. Yeah, bye."

She turned and gave Alyssa a smile. "Hey, hon, have a good time?"

A smile crept up onto Alyssa's face, despite the caution she felt at overhearing the phone conversation. "I did. Wendy even let me ride one of the horses."

"Oh, that's wonderful!" Jessica clapped her hands before wrapping Alyssa into a bear-hug. "We'll have to go get you a pair of riding boots then!"

The smile faded. "Oh, um. I don't want to be an imposition."

Jessica walked around to the driver's door and slid into the car. "You will never be an imposition," she responded as Alyssa buckled her seatbelt.

She wanted to believe her, but the phone conversation kept replaying in her head. Deep down, she knew there was something big that Jessica wasn't telling her, something vital to her existence. All she could do was hope that the ball didn't drop before she was ready to take her life into her own hands.

Twenty-One

"You okay?" Brianna whispered from her seat beside Alyssa.

It had been two weeks since the incident at the coffee shop and she still felt rattled, waiting for "it" to happen, for Jessica to finally realize what a huge mistake she was making. The doubts scattered in the light of day, especially during her time at Bayberry when she and Jessica worked side by side cleaning and feeding the horses. Yet, in the dark of midnight, the voices inside her head pushed for her to run, to leave on her own accord instead of being forced out of the house like so many times in the past, reminding her that it could all just be ripped away with no notice.

"Yep," she replied dryly, opening her science book and swallowing down the urge to tell her friend everything.

Caleb slid into his desk just as the bell rang and flicked Alyssa's short pony-tail with his hand. "Don't believe that lie. She's not okay, but won't tell anyone what's wrong."

"Leave me alone," she hissed, frustrated at the tears that sprang to her eyes, a sign that she was unable to keep a tight rein on her emotions as she could in the past.

Then the teacher began to speak, and she was suddenly filled with relief that she could finally force the emotions from her mind, could just focus on the book in front of her.

I'm going to beat this, she kept repeating every time her attention shifted. *I am going to rise above. I am not going to drop out of high school. I am going to college. I am going to have a good life. I don't need anyone. I'm fine on my own.*

A slip of paper slid under her elbow and she dropped the note into her lap before the teacher sensed its presence. Ms. Davison had a habit of always keeping her back to the room, fully engrossed in the diagrams or images she presented along with the lesson, but she could never be too safe.

Never gonna happen

Her brows furrowed in confusion at the note. *What's never going to happen? Getting out of here? Having a good life? How did he get into my head?* The hair on her neck prickled as indignation slowly burned through her body. Another note plopped on her lap, dropped from over her shoulder.

Leaving you alone, that is. Stuck with us 4eva. Remember?

Concentration broken, she crumpled the notes and dropped them back over her shoulder onto Caleb's desk. She spent the rest of the lesson ignoring the feeling of his fingers twirling her ponytail, or the whispers of Brianna and Caleb talking about her.

It was better before I knew them, she thought determinedly. *It was better with no friends, no one to hurt me.* What was she thinking when she started to let her guard slip, to let people in? Darren had come over a few nights ago, after she had already gone to her room to finish homework, and she could hear him and Jessica arguing. After the confrontation with the couple, she knew it was about her.

It's all falling apart. A tear splashed onto her science book as the final bell of the day rang. Alyssa shoved her book into her backpack and jumped up, darting to the front of the room before her friends had a chance to gather their items.

Caleb pushed through the students until he was at her side, Brianna clinging to his backpack to ride through the path he created. "Alli, stop."

"Alyssa, talk to us." Brianna reached out to catch Alyssa's shoulder, but she just pulled away faster, ignoring both of them.

"We're not leaving you alone you know," Caleb warned, easily staying two steps behind her as Alyssa dodged through the hallway. Minutes later, they were outside, and Alyssa adjusted her backpack on her shoulder, preparing to run.

Caleb knew, and reached out his hand to stop her. "You can't get rid of us that easily." His fingers wrapped around one of the worn flaps of her backpack, and tugged back as she moved forward.

The tearing noise filled the air as Alyssa spun around. "Just leave me alone. Stop trying to put me back together when I'm already shattered past repair." Then her books crashed onto the sidewalk as the fabric of her backpack unraveled, so thin from a lifetime of use that it could no longer hold the weight of her world.

For a moment, everything was still. They stared at the pile of books and the paper-thin fabric that was now fluttering on her back in the cold breeze like a warning flag. Caleb broke the stillness, bending down to pick up Alyssa's school books and lift them in a neat pile. Brianna grabbed the pencil case and the copies of Alyssa's favorite books and a small stuffed cat.

Alyssa stood in shock, moving her backpack to her hand as she felt her heart rip in two. Then she snatched away the items from Brianna, yelled, "Just let me be alone!" and ran away from their help and their love.

~ * ~ * ~

She burst through the front door, her blurred vision briefly passing over the hazy shapes of Jessica and Darren as she ran through to her room.

"Alli, what's -" Jessica began, the chair scraping as she stood.

"Just leave me alone!" Alyssa yelled before slamming her door shut. Her forehead fell against the smooth wood as she pushed the lock in, breaking the cardinal rule of every house in which she had ever lived. The sobs started, slowly at first, a sniffle as the tears continued to well in her eyes. Then they rose in earnest, great heaving sobs that shook her body as she crawled over to her closet and pulled her body inside, burying herself in clothes while she curled over the pile of fabric that used to be her backpack, her only consistency over the last six years.

It was a mistake letting them in, the voice told her as she sobbed. *Better to love? Yeah right. Better to be cold, emotionless, never yielding. Every time you give someone a chance, they take you away. Every time you think the bad times are over, they just get worse. Curl up into a ball and give up, little girl, because this hole is the best you are ever going to get, the best you deserve.*

"No," she whimpered, moving her hands to cover her ears in an attempt to block out the voice. "No, it's going to get better."

Ha! It replied. *That's what you've been saying for six years, and where has it gotten you? Your heart has been crushed more times than you can count, your body violated, your will sapped. Why keep fighting? No one cares if one little kid disappears. It would mean less money for taxpayers, less time at work for the social workers. Jessica would have her life back. You are an insignificant little nothing, and you know it.*

"Stop it!" she yelled, hiccuping and breathless as she banged her palms against her head.

The sound of yelling in the living room silenced the voice in her head, and her body froze at the sound of a door slamming followed by deliberate footsteps walking toward her room. Her body curled itself tighter involuntarily, eyes scrunched shut and her back pushing deeper into the closet as her lungs fought for air.

"Alli?" There was a small scraping sound, then a popping as the lock on the door was pushed into the unlocked position and the knob turned. Quick footsteps crossed the room and then she was wrapped in soft, strong arms. The scent of flowers suddenly draped around her like a curtain, and she inhaled deeply, vaguely aware that someone was speaking beyond her desolate world.

"Sweetheart, come back to me. Whatever happened, we will work through it together. You aren't alone anymore, Alyssa. Let me in, honey. Let me help you." The voice pushed the stars away, sweet yet firm; it caused Alyssa's heart to yearn for more, to trust it, to let it in.

Her voice was hoarse as she whispered, "I don't want to wreck your life like I ruined my mom's."

Surprise filled Jessica's tone. "You haven't, Alli, and you won't, not ever. Why would you think that?"

Alyssa cracked her eyes opened and felt more hot tears race down her cheeks. "That day, the couple in the coffee shop. They were right. I'll just destroy your life."

"No, they were not." The fierceness and anger that filled Jessica's voice jolted Alyssa into full awareness. "I knew your mother well, Alyssa, and you are nothing like her. You have already brought richness to my life that I never imagined would be here. This *will* be your last home, and you will always be welcome here, understood?"

"What do you mean, you knew my mother? Does that mean you know where she is? Does the couple from the coffee shop know? Why didn't you tell me?" Alyssa felt her skin prickle, unsure if it was anger or fear.

"I don't know where she is, sweetheart." Jessica hesitated, blowing a puff of air out that caused her hair to flutter. "I knew your mom when I was younger, before she had you. I haven't talked to her in over a decade. I didn't tell you because I didn't think it would help, and you had enough on your plate with moving and starting a new school and didn't need any extra stress."

"Oh," Alyssa whispered, feeling the brief moment of rebellion fade back into complacency, back to the place where her heart was protected by thick walls. Her finger ran over the torn edge of the backpack and she began to cry anew, too tired and emotionally drained to ask more questions.

Jessica gently pulled the fabric from Alyssa's hand and gave a sad sigh. "Come on, sweetie. Let's go get you washed up, and then we'll see if we can put this back together."

"Do you think it can be mended?" Alyssa whispered, remembering the look of shock and fear on the faces of her friends as she yelled and ran.

Jessica studied the backpack. "It won't be exactly the same, no. But I think we can figure out a way to patch this up, or maybe to turn it into something else, if you need a new backpack. Come on, let's go give it a try together."

Twenty-Two

Saturday dawned clear and cold, and Alyssa spent a long time just watching the thin branches of the tree outside swaying in the wind. Her head still pounded, her body aching from the emotions that had raced through over the past forty-eight hours.

Jessica had taken one look at her the morning after her breakdown and told her to stay in bed, even though it meant missing school. Alyssa had been crying off and on again for the entire day, as if the emotions that had begun to flow were unable to be pushed back into the box where she kept them safely contained.

She felt gross, her hair stringy and body sticky from the sweat that accompanied her nightmares the night before. A vague memory of Jessica cradling her while she cried caused a blush to creep up her cheeks, and Alyssa was almost grateful that she could rarely remember the dreams once daylight came.

A deep breath, then she pushed off the covers and swung her feet over the edge, feeling stronger; at least, strong enough for a shower.

The hot water blasted her head and she took another breath, the steam clearing the heavy feeling from her lungs and lightening her spirits. Alyssa took her time in the shower, carefully washing her hair and soaping her body, then just stood in the water as she gathered the strength to step out and greet the day.

The house was quiet, and she immediately spotted a note from Jessica on the kitchen counter, next to a plate of pancakes that were still warm.

Emergency at work. Be home around 3. Caleb stopped by but I told him you were asleep. Don't leave him hanging.

After happily eating the pancakes, which Jessica had sprinkled with white chocolate chips, and replacing the sweat-dampened bedding with fresh sheets, Alyssa curled up on the couch and stared at her cell phone. She had never yelled at anyone before, not in six years, not after she realized there was so much at stake if she lost control. Now she had actively tried to push away the three people in her life who acted like they cared.

Okay. She fiddled with the phone, flipping it open and closed as her nerves jittered through her fingers. *Worst case, they don't want to be your friend anymore. Been there, done that. You can deal with it. Just get it done.*

She started with Brianna, opting for a text so that she would not have to actually hear the rejection.

I'm sorry I acted crazy. Want to come over and play with Tulip tomorrow?

While she waited for the reply, certain that Brianna would still be asleep for several more hours, she texted Caleb.

I'm sorry

She hit send, and her fingers hovered on the buttons, wanting to explain more, needing him to accept the apology, but terrified of taking it further and facing rejection.

Several minutes later, a knock sounded on the front door, and there stood Caleb, hands tucked into his pockets. "Want to go take a walk around the pond?"

Alyssa nodded, silent as she grabbed her coat and stuffed her wallet and cell phone into her pant pockets. Her hand hesitated on the strap of her backpack, still hanging in its place by the door, but then she released it, her lifeline now only a pile of fabric until she and Jess could figure out some way to bring it back to life.

They rode in silence, Caleb tapping his fingers on the steering wheel and Alyssa staring out the glass window, terrified of what he would say. Houses flashed by, children bundled up in coats playing in their yards, enjoying their day.

He parked, and they walked to the pond, finally sitting on the small bench under a barren oak tree that overlooked the small cove where the ducks who had forgotten to fly south gathered.

"Caleb, I'm sorry." Alyssa pulled her legs up and hugged her knees to her chest.

His lips twitched. "You said that already."

"Can we still be friends?"

A snort broke the heavy stillness of the air and he draped his arm around her, pulling Alyssa closer to him on the bench. "Oh come on, give me some credit! You've got to do more than just yell at me to get rid of me. I mean, maybe like, if you set me on fire or stabbed me with a rusty nail or something ..."

Relieved laughter bubbled from Alyssa as she playfully punched his shoulder, pushing away from his body and looking at the ducks. "Why are you so nice to me when I'm such a psycho?"

There was a long pause as Caleb took a cigarette from his pack and lit it. "Well, from where I stand, you need a person that you can be mean to, be psycho around, and that person is just going to have be me."

Brown eyes rolled and Alyssa fought the urge to knock the white stick out of his mouth. "Because that makes any sense at all."

Caleb just stared at her a long moment before turning his head to blow the smoke away from her. "Alli, everyone needs someone to be mean to sometimes. You have spent your entire life being nice, being perfect, so careful never to offend or upset anyone. It's all bottled up in there, a lifetime of hurt and anger, both big and little, never able to be released because of your fear that it will ruin your life. It's important for every person to have someone who will always forgive them, always love them, no matter what. For you, that person is me. No matter how mean you are, or how badly you screw something up, I'm not going anywhere, because I know that it's not who you are. When the stress of being perfect becomes too much to bear, I'll be there to catch you, no strings attached."

Alyssa's heart swelled, but her mind was filled with warning bells. "Caleb, you know that …"

A wink had her heart more at ease. "Oh, quiet you. That's not a proposal or anything. Goody two-shoes aren't my type."

"Oh, shut up." Her eyes rolled again and she gave him friendly nudge, then moved her hand to knock the cigarette out of his fingers.

"That's more like it!" He pushed her hand away, then, after a final drag, went and dropped the cigarette in the nearest public ashtray.

Alyssa sat with her legs crossed on the bench and cocked her head as he approached. "You know those are bad for you, right?"

"I had no idea," he said sarcastically. "So is shutting your friends out when you need them the most."

"I'll stop if you will." The words were out before she realized what she was saying, and she immediately felt guilty. What he did with his body was none of her business, and she waited for him to verbally slap her down.

Instead he pulled the half-full pack out of his pocket and stared at it a long moment. "Deal," he quietly agreed, walking to the nearest trash can and dropping the cardboard box into the mesh circle. "But you are going to have to deal with a major crank-ass with the last name of Rose, and I want something from you in return."

"Okay." Her voice was timid, remembering the other times when someone wanted something from her. It was always something different, but always bad. Jay was the worst, the only assault on her body, but there had been other requests, corroborating lies, covering tracks, hiding drugs, giving money.

Caleb sat back down and watched the ducks as he gave her time to settle, as if he knew she was being battered by the past and was giving her time to come back to the present. "Promise me that no matter how mad you are at me, or sad, or upset in any degree, you will answer my texts or calls. Even if it's just a simple, 'kay,' don't leave me hanging. My mind goes to bad places."

A duck moved across the cold pond surface, gliding from the protection of one group of rocks to another. "That's it?" she asked.

"Yep." He paused and looked down as his phone began to go off, the heavy-metal ringtone jarring the peace of the pond. "That would be Bri. Do you need more time to be alone, or are you ready to go join sleeping beauty at the diner?"

"Lunch would be great. Let's go."

Twenty-Three

"Pleeeease, Alyssa," Brianna drew out the words. "Please, please, pleeeeease, come on a double date this weekend with me. Please!"

"Because the last two went so well?" Alyssa glared at Brianna and returned to stabbing at her fruit cup with her fork. Brianna had convinced her to start going on double dates with her a month ago, and the experience did not bode well for Alyssa's future.

"I said I'm sorry! I didn't think they were that bad. I'll warn this guy to keep his hands off you." She took a sip of her soda and handed Alyssa a spoon.

Alyssa grunted her thanks as she scooped the slippery fruit bits onto the spoon. After begging from Brianna and encouragement from Jessica, she had agreed to give dating a try. With Devon, they were only ten minutes into the fair ride before his hands were on her leg. During the dinner with Trevor, he kept insisting that Alyssa try his food, and kept moving so that his body was always touching hers, even when she edged away so far that she almost fell off the booth seat.

"I'm sorry too, Bri. I'm just broken when it comes to physical contact. You know that." Deep down,

Alyssa wondered if she would ever be able to form a romantic relationship with a guy. How did romance happen when your skin crawled from people trying to give an innocent hug?

She looked up and saw Brianna holding out a piece of white chocolate as a bribe. "Please come? We're planning on doing something totally cheesy, like painting your own pottery or something. I promise. No dark places or tight quarters."

Caleb's voice chimed in from behind, "And if he lays one hand on you, I'll make sure he never so much as looks at you again."

Water trickled down Alyssa's throat as she gasped in surprise, causing her to sputter and cough. "Yeah, okay, Dad."

"Brother," he responded gruffly as he sat down beside her and inhaled a cheeseburger.

"What?" both girls inquired in tandem, confused about both the conversation and his abrupt mood.

"I'm your brother, not your father." His voice was rough and his leg jittered under the table as he ate.

"Duh," Brianna chimed in.

"Obviously you aren't my father, seeing as how he's probably living in Hawaii with his dream family after dumping the unwanted baggage." The words came out light, but seeing Caleb flinch brought a weight upon them for which Alyssa was not prepared.

"Caleb," she spoke tentatively, "you okay?"

"I don't want to talk about it." His gray eyes flashed a warning to back off, a warning that Alyssa immediately ignored.

"You never give me that option." She bumped her knee against his, temporarily stopping the bouncing. "Hey, jitterbug, what's up?"

His fingers gripped her knee and briefly squeezed. "Somebody convinced me give up smoking and it sucks. That's what up."

"Not buying it, what else?" Head cocked to the side, Alyssa saw the muscles jumping in his chin and throat.

"Drop it, Alyssa," he growled.

"Nope."

"I said, drop it." His fist clenched and unclenched on the table, twisting and crushing his plastic fork.

"And I said, no." Alyssa met his eyes steadily, for once unafraid of an angry male. She knew he would never hurt her, and remembered what he said about pushing away those you love.

His eyes dropped the gaze first and he mumbled, "I'll tell you later."

"Me too?" Brianna asked softly.

Alyssa gave a subtle nod and Caleb grunted agreement. They had made a pact to keep as much stress and bleakness away from Brianna as possible until she got her feet back under her, but Alyssa had a feeling this was big, and Caleb needed everything they could give.

~ * ~ * ~

They sat in Alyssa's room, Caleb looking masculine and out of place surrounded by turquoise and gray. He was slumped on the floor, back against the wall and eyes closed. Alyssa sat on the bed next to Brianna, Tulip curled up between them as the kitten vibrated Alyssa's leg with her purring.

"My mom is in the hospital," Caleb started, and Alyssa swallowed hard at the shakiness of his voice. "She finally saw my dad hit me, and she stepped in. For the first time since I can remember, she tried to stop him from hitting me again, and he turned on her."

"Oh, Caleb," Alyssa whispered as she saw him shudder. Tulip immediately jumped off the bed and onto his lap, purring and rubbing her face against the stubble on Caleb's chin.

His voice hoarse, he continued. "He told the hospital that someone broke into our house and beat her up because she wouldn't give them money. The doctor said that she has a broken cheek-bone, three cracked ribs, shattered knee cap, and fractured pelvis. I don't think the doc believed it for a second, but since Mom confirmed the story, there's nothing he can do. My father told me to keep my mouth shut, or he'd give us both worse beatings next time, and my sister too."

A tear slipped from his eye, and Alyssa heard Brianna suck in a breath beside her.

"Caleb," Alyssa said as she slid from the bed and pressed her body next to his. "You're going to get through this. Stay here tonight, and maybe you can convince your mom to change her story. Where is your sister?"

"She was visiting my grandparents this week, so she's safe, she's ..."

Brianna followed suit and hopped off the bed, curling herself to Caleb's other side. "I don't even know what to say, but we're here for you, no matter what."

His arms wrapped around both of them and held on tightly as he cried, and Alyssa and Brianna shared a worried look at the depth of his pain. He was the unflappable one that they leaned on when they needed help, the one who always made sure they were safe, happy, and felt loved.

Finally the storm blew over, and he accepted the box of tissues that Alyssa had pulled over from her bed. She gave his hand a squeeze and then stood up. "I'm going to go talk to Jess. I'll be back. You two entertain Tulip."

The hallway felt as if it grew longer with every step that Alyssa took toward the living room. Jessica was sitting at her desk, looking through ledgers filled with numbers and making notations every few pages. Alyssa slightly cleared her throat and shifted her weight as Jessica put down her pencil and turned in the chair.

"What's up, Alli?" Her hair was pulled into a loose bun, but pieces that had fallen out framed her face, curling slightly at the tips.

She looks stressed, and sad, Alyssa thought, feeling guilty for the question she was about to ask. She had never asked for anything this important before, had never even asked for a sleepover, and was terrified the answer would be no, or a trip back to the social worker's office.

"Um, would it be possible for Caleb to spend the next night or two here?" Her voice quivered as she asked, so quietly that, at first, Alyssa wasn't sure if Jessica had even heard her.

Jessica just raised an eyebrow and looked toward the bedroom, where Brianna had started giggling. "Explain."

"I, I can't. Not really. It's just," she took a deep breath, "there are some bad things going on at his house, and his sister is with their grandparents, and his mom is in the hospital, so it's just him and his dad, and it would really mean a lot of he could stay here a couple of days, on the couch, of course." The words came out quickly, pushing together as if she had to expel them before they became stuck in her throat forever.

Jessica continued to stare at her silently, and just as Alyssa began to feel sweat trickling down her neck, Caleb walked out of her bedroom.

Hands in his pockets and head low, he mumbled, "Don't worry about it, Ms. Sona. I'll be fine."

She held up a hand, then gestured to the couch. "I haven't said no yet, but I need more information. Why is your mom in the hospital, and will your dad have the cops banging at my door if you don't go home?"

Alyssa watched silently as Caleb licked his lips and fiddled with the chain he used as a belt. She knew he had low regard for trusting adults, almost as low as her own, and silently begged for him to trust Jessica, just this once.

"My mom," he hesitated, squared his shoulders, then continued. "My mom was hurt last night, and is going to be in the hospital for a few days in observation. I don't know if it's safe to be at home right now, but I don't want to get her into any trouble by telling anyone that. I already called my grandparents, and Trixie can stay there for a while, but I'm not welcome. We don't exactly have a good relationship."

Nodding slowly, Jessica chewed on the tip of her pen for a moment. "What would your father say if he knew you were staying here?"

"Nothing." Caleb shrugged. "He went straight from the hospital to the bar to 'de-stress.' If anything, he's probably still in a drunken stupor at a friend's house."

"Okay, I will let you crash here on one condition." Jessica looked at both teens sternly. "One, there is absolutely no drugs, alcohol, or hanky-panky in this house, period. Two," her eyes softened, "Caleb, I trust you, but you need to let your dad know where you are, in some fashion. I don't want police showing up here thinking I kidnapped you, okay?"

He gave an indifferent shrug, but Alyssa saw the sheen that started to form on his eyes. "Will do. I'll just text him that I'm at a friend's house. That's always been enough for him." Caleb turned away to walk back down the hallway, Brianna waiting at Alyssa's door. Once he reached the door, he turned back and gave a small smile. "Thank you, Ms. Sona. I promise I won't make you regret this."

Alyssa felt her heart swell as Jessica just smiled at the teens and said, "Please, call me Jessica."

Twenty-Four

Caleb looked so out of place leaning against the barn in his baggy black jeans and combat boots that Alyssa couldn't help but giggle. She was surprised at his eagerness to accompany her and Jessica to Bayberry for their volunteer day, but supposed it was better than staying on the couch, alone, until they got back.

"It's quieter here when there isn't a classroom of teens," he commented, pushing off the wall to follow Alyssa down the aisle to where the rakes and buckets were stored.

"Just a little bit." She smiled as she agreed, taking in a deep breath of the fresh alfalfa hay in the feed room to her right. "It gets busier on lesson days, but today it's just other volunteers and the couple of workers cleaning up, so it's really peaceful."

"Mhm." His eyebrow raised in disbelief. "Only you would think cleaning horse poop was peaceful."

"It is," Alyssa insisted as she picked up two muck-rakes and moved a bucket over to the first empty stall. "You don't have to really think about what you are doing, so you can just kind of, drift. And it's actually really gratifying to be able to clean a stall, immediate satisfaction and all that."

Both teens were in the stall when they heard a high-pitched voice call out, "Heads up for Cheeky!"

"Oh, boy," Alyssa ducked her head into the hallway and started laughing at the sight of the miniature horse cantering down the aisle, nylon halter held in his teeth.

He flew past, short legs pumping and mane flying, only to come to a sliding halt in front of where Jessica stood at the end of the aisle. One hand rested on her hip, and the other came up, index finger pointed at the pony.

"Now, Cheeky, what have we said about taking these trips on your own?" Jessica smiled at the horse, who gave her a nicker in response. "Come on, back we go." He stood docilely as she slipped a halter over his head, latched the buckle, and led him back to his stall.

Caleb pulled the bucket filled with soiled sawdust into the aisle and shook his head. "She's certainly turned into the horse whisperer, hasn't she?"

"Ooooh yes," agreed Alyssa. "They all love her, even Yuda, and he doesn't like anybody."

They moved into the next stall, both working quietly at scooping the manure and clumped sawdust into the bucket and smoothing new sawdust over the area. Jessica's laugh filled the barn, and Caleb poked his head out of the stall.

"What's Mr. Sanders doing here?"

Alyssa carefully re-did her ponytail and took a swig of water from her bottle before answering. "Oh, he comes here every other weekend to volunteer. They've both been working a lot with Yuda, trying to get him to come out of his depression, and he's actually pretty cool. You know, for a teacher."

Mr. Sanders came down the aisle a few minutes later, leading Yuda, whose eyes sparkled a little more each day, and stepped carefully into the riding ring. Jessica followed behind, leading Thunder and holding two hard black-velvet safety helmets in her hand.

"Come on, Alli. We're going to see if some exercise will help Yuda perk up a bit more, and Wendy thought it would help if you and Thunder rode with us." She held out the helmet to Alyssa, who took it with a backward glance at Caleb.

"Go on," he said, shooing her. "I'll finish up here and then come watch."

She stepped out of the stall, taking her place by Thunder's head and leading him over to the mounting block. While she was able to manage holding him still while mounting, her legs were not yet strong enough to pull herself onto the tall horse's back from the ground, so the help of the raised platform was a necessity.

Alyssa took a moment to sit on his back, checking the stirrup length before slipping her feet from the metal stirrups and rolling her ankles in circles to warm them up. Carefully holding the reins the way that Wendy showed, she gently nudged the gelding with her calves, grinning when Thunder moved into a smooth walk and she was able to hold her balance.

"Excellent job, Alli. I didn't even see you tell him to do that this time," Wendy called out from the center of the ring.

A grin spread across Alyssa's face as she slid her feet into the stirrups, then gently nudged the horse into a trot. She had been terrified the first time Wendy had encouraged her to try the faster gait, bouncing around on his back like an unwieldy sack of onions, but had quickly settled into his rhythm, her body moving with his pace.

"Heels down a little more, that's better. Okay, Jess, let's see if Yuda will trot for you."

Jessica's joyous laugh of success carried across the ring, and Alyssa looked behind her to see Yuda happily trotting after Thunder, his shorter legs flying to keep pace with Thunder's longer, slender limbs.

"Easy, you. Slow it down now," Jessica quietly encouraged the horse, lightly tugging on the reins and bringing Yuda's pace back down to a slower, smoother gait. "You aren't a racehorse you know, you silly boy."

Together, they spent an hour riding around the sandy ring, alternating between walking and trotting, even breaking into an accidental, terrifying, and exhilarating canter. At one point, Alyssa glanced over, worried that Caleb would be bored sitting on the bench, and was happily surprised to see him engrossed in conversation with Mr. Sanders, their teacher who had also started volunteering after the field trip.

"Alright, ladies. That's it for today. Let's get these boys back in and give them the rub-down they deserve." Wendy moved toward them, standing beside the horses as Jessica and Alyssa swung their legs over and dropped down. The first time, both had stumbled and landed on their backs in the sand, laughing until tears rolled down their cheeks as the horses investigated their clumsy humans. Now, they were able to gracefully dismount, rolling up their stirrups and loosening the horses' girths before leading them back to their stalls.

As they passed by, Alyssa heard Mr. Sanders turn to Caleb and say, "Jessica has really worked wonders with Yuda. We were worried he had given up on life and wondering if he was going to make it, but now, it's like he has hope again."

She paused beside them, watching Yuda push his muzzle into Jessica's hand as she led the horse down the aisle. "Yeah, Jessica is really good at fixing broken things and giving them back hope."

Twenty-Five

Outside Alyssa's window, a car door slammed, pulling her attention away from the index cards scattered on the floor between her and Caleb.

He continued looking through the cards, oblivious. "Why are you making me study this again?"

"Because you need to pass this test to pass the course to graduate," Alyssa replied, her heart rate increasing as she glanced down to the street and saw the black-and-white police car parked in front of the house.

"And I care about graduating why?" Caleb looked at another flash card before flicking it into the air and watching it gently float back down.

"Because you and I are going to make something with our lives, despite what everyone around us says." Alyssa watched as two cops stepped out of the car and walked up the driveway. "Caleb, there are -" She was cut off by the sound of a door knocking.

"Alli, can you get that? I'm still getting ready for tonight," Jessica's voice came through the bathroom door, along with the smell of her new lavender shampoo.

"Um, okay, but it's the cops."

"What?" Jessica's voice became strangled. "I'll be there in half a second."

Alyssa walked down the hallway, feeling as if every step was taking her closer to her doom. It was rare that the cops showed up; normally it was the social workers, so she was equally afraid for herself and for Caleb.

Straightening her shoulders, she opened the door a crack and put on a smile. "Good afternoon, officers. How can we help you?"

The uniformed officer discretely looked around through the crack and gave a stern smile. "Good afternoon, is there an adult available?"

Jessica quickly opened the door and edged Alyssa to the side. "Yes, hello. What can we do for you? Oh, hello, Eric."

The younger officer gave a genuine smile. "Hey, Jess. Is this a bad time?"

Isn't it always when you show up? Alyssa thought, keeping a happy face pasted on out of habit. It was obvious that Jessica had been caught unprepared for company. While she was fully dressed in her navy-blue flared skirt and black lace halter top, her hair was still wrapped in the rose-colored towel from her shower.

"Not at all. What can we help you gentlemen with?"

"Do you know a boy named Caleb Rose? He's a high-schooler around here." The question was asked innocently enough, but Alyssa felt a stone drop into her stomach.

"I do," Jessica answered smoothly. "What do you need to know about Caleb?"

The officers shared a look, and the older turned to walk to the car while the younger remained at the door. "Jess, we need to find his whereabouts, and all we've got is a text message saying that he's staying with a friend. We were hoping that maybe you've seen him around town and would know something, or maybe which friend he was with at the moment."

"He'll probably be at school tomorrow. That would be an easy enough way to find him." Jessica kept her voice neutral, and Alyssa motioned, behind her back, for Caleb to stop walking down the hallway to see what was going on.

Eric rubbed the back of his neck. "I shouldn't be telling you this, but his mom got beat up pretty badly. She freaked when she got home and Caleb wasn't there, called us, and started telling us a very different version of the story than she told the hospital. We're hoping if we find the kid, we can get the true story. She is also going crazy with worry, saying that his father must have killed him and we need to lock him up for murder."

Caleb appeared behind Alyssa and stepped between Jessica, who shrugged, and the officer. "Where is my mom? What did she tell you?"

"Mr. Rose, I need you to come to the station with us." The younger cop stiffened and his partner quickly walked back to the door from his position next to the car.

Each word emphasized, Caleb repeated, "Where is my mother?"

"She is at the station as well. Now come with us, please."

He looked back at Alyssa and swallowed hard. "Alright, let me grab my bag real quick. Alyssa, can you help me pack up my homework?"

"Sure," she answered automatically, trying hard not to send a puzzled look his way.

They walked down the hallway, and he sat down on her bed with a heavy thud. "Do you think she actually talked?"

Alyssa sat down beside him and tucked her feet under her. "I don't know, but I guess it's possible. Call me later?"

"Will do. See ya. And, Alli? Thanks, for everything."

~ * ~ * ~

Need 2 talk. Meet at park?

Alyssa quickly texted an affirmative response and grabbed her hoodie from the chair by her door.

"Hey, Jess, do you mind if I go to the park and talk to Caleb?"

"Sure, hon. Be home before dark though, okay?" Jessica kept her eyes focused on the rapidly moving text on the phone in front her.

Alyssa heard a deep sigh from her keeper, who she was starting to really feel more like an aunt than just a temporary guardian, as she stepped out the door, newly sewn purse in hand.

It was Jessica's creativity that brought Alyssa's lifeline back, turning her backpack into a bag large enough to hold all of her essential items, like her few pictures, her two favorite books, and her diary, but still small enough to pass as a purse. Her keeper had painstakingly cut around the seams of the bag, salvaging as much fabric as possible and then reinforcing it with a sturdy plastic frame. She had even taken one of the shirts that Alyssa loved so much, but was no longer able to wear after her last growth spurt, and used that to sew the lining.

A bag of love and light and hope, Alyssa thought, mentally repeating Jessica's words as she felt warmth fill her heart.

The air was brisk, but even in the hours before sunset, she felt the promise of spring. All of the snow remaining from the last winter storm had fully melted back into the earth and tiny flowers dotted the landscape, creating tiny spots of color, causing Alyssa to smile as she walked along the sidewalk to the park.

I hope this isn't bad news, she thought as she dropped her hood, reveling in the sunshine upon her hair. It had only been a few hours since they had taken Caleb to the station, and she was scared, not only for him, but for his mom and sister as well.

That was the one horror of foster care that she had never been faced with, physical abuse. Well, with the exception of Jay, but others had received so much worse. She could not even imagine what thoughts were going through the minds of her friend and his mother, both beaten by his father, both terrified for one another and his innocent sister. Terrified enough to cover it all up.

Then the park was in front of her, and she saw the black hoodie with the white skull that Caleb loved so much. He was sitting on a bench, his eyes sweeping back and forth, watching children as they ran and slid.

"Hey, Caleb." Alyssa slid onto the bench next to him and linked her arm through his, wanting him to know she was there for him. "What happened?"

His head dropped, and strands of long brown hair fell from behind the hood. "She told them everything." Caleb's voice was gravely, strained, and he gave a low, long breath before continuing. "When she got home and saw I was gone, she assumed the worst, especially when my grandparents said they had Trixie but not me. My father wasn't there, which was lucky for both of us. She immediately went to the station and told them everything. Everything he had done to her. Everything he had done to me. Lucky for both of us, I still had the bruises from last time, so they didn't need too much convincing."

Alyssa sucked in a breath as he leaned back against the bench and pushed the hood and hair from around his face. "What now?"

A hint of a smile played across his face. "He's in jail. It turns out we weren't the only people he had threatened in this town, and others had filed reports about him, things like bar skirmishes that were dismissed because of his 'outstanding citizenship.' There's a restraining order against him too, if he comes near Mom or Trixie or me once he gets out."

"Are you happy? That's good, right?" She treaded lightly, not willing to push him, not wanting to push herself.

Caleb blinked, then licked his lips. "I don't know. I feel like I should be. I'm relieved that we don't have to deal with his B.S. anymore, but it's kind of unsettling not knowing what's going to happen in the next few weeks."

"Yeah, change is terrifying, even when you know it's for the best," Alyssa commiserated.

"It's like, at least his anger was constant. I knew what set him off, and what would shut him up. Devil-you-know, you know?"

She stared at the children on the monkey bars. "Yeah, I get that."

"Is this how you feel about your mom? I heard you crying the other night, in your sleep. I didn't understand how you could want her back, but now ... I think I get it."

Her stomach clenched as if she had been punched and Alyssa pulled away from him on the bench, needing some space. "Yeah. Something like that."

"Alli - " Caleb scooted her way, pushing her toward the end of the bench.

"This isn't about me, Caleb. We're talking about your dad remember?" *Shallow breaths. Don't go there, Caleb*, she silently pleaded.

He scooted down the bench until she was at the very edge. "That's about it. He's probably going to stay in jail, Mom will be fine. Now I need a distraction from my crap. Is that what it's like with your mom? I'm not stopping until you tell me."

"Yeah, it is, just like that," she snapped as she jumped up and stood in front of him on the bench. "Sure, she said she hated me, and she yelled at me, and I always felt like I wasn't good enough, but at least I knew what was going on. I knew what I did that made her mad, and sad, and could just file them away as things I should never do again. One day, I would have figured out what made her happy, and then we would have just been fine. I just didn't have enough time to figure out how to be the daughter she wanted."

Alyssa felt her skin began to flush and wrapped her arms around her torso. "I'd be better at it now, better at getting her to love me. If she would just come back, I could make it work. I'd give anything for her to come back. She would see me, and we would cry, and she would beg for me to forgive her for making a mistake and then take me home. I'd have my family back."

He just looked at her with his gray eyes before slowly rubbing the back of his neck. "What would that do to Jess?"

"She'd get over it." Alyssa swallowed hard, staring over his shoulder, at the tree, anywhere but his eyes because they saw too much.

"You really think that? She loves you."

"Drop it, Caleb," she choked out. "You don't know what it's like to never know if your parent is going to just give you away like a freaking stray puppy. Oh look, the puppy peed on the couch again, time to send it back to the shelter and get a better one. When Jessica gets sick of me, I'll be right back at square one. How did this become about me? I'm so sick of talking about myself. I'm not important, so stop poking at me and making me seem like someone worth keeping."

"You keep harping on that, you know." This time it was Caleb who was heated. He paused, took a moment to control himself as he saw a few adults look their way, then stood up and nudged Alyssa toward the parking lot.

"It's true." Her voice shook as she fought for control, matching her steps to his as they walked to his truck.

"Yeah, I know. It's true for the others, but not for Jess. She doesn't abandon people like that. She's not your mom."

Alyssa slid into the truck and slammed the door, clenching her eyes shut to push back the tears. She heard Caleb slide in beside her and let out a shuddery breath. "That's what I thought about the second house, and the fourth, and the ninth. That's what I thought every damn time I let someone in, and look at what happened, Caleb. When they got sick of me, or things got tight, they passed me off like a used pair of jeans. I'm nothing, to everyone."

She looked over and saw his jaw clenching, the muscle jumping under the stubble of his unshaven chin. He glanced at her, bit his lip and opened his mouth to speak, then shut it again. A swallow, and then he tried again. "Jessica isn't like the others, okay? She's …" he faltered, slamming his hand against the steering wheel in frustration. "Damn it. She's just not, trust me on this one."

Head back, eyes focused on the cloth roof to hold back tears, Alyssa just nodded. "Sure, she's not like them. Remember that when I just disappear one day."

Twenty-Six

Brianna promised cheesy, Alyssa thought wryly, *and cheesy this is.* She gave her friend a sideways look as the car driven by Brianna's date pulled into the parking lot of a local petting zoo. Alyssa's date for the day, a senior at the school named Josh, slid out of the backseat beside her and then held open the door.

"Welcome to the Apple Ridge Zoo!" Jeremy said with a huge grin and wide sweep of his hands. "This is going to be awesome."

Alyssa's eyes slid over to Josh, and a giggle escaped at the look of utter disbelief on his face. The giggle caught his attention, and he looked back, his shoulders beginning to shake as he tried to hold in the laughter.

"Oh, sure. Laugh now," Brianna pointed a finger at the two of them, "but you just wait."

Josh held up his hands in surrender. "Alright, we'll reserve judgment until after we get head-butted in the butt by a little goat."

Alyssa was surprised at the genuine warmth of his words, and felt a small blush creep onto her cheeks as he held open the door to the entrance for her as she stepped through. "Um, thanks."

"No prob, bob. Ready to pretend we're eight again?" His smile was infectious, but faltered when Alyssa paled at his words.

"Yeah, right. Let's go." She didn't want to admit that she had never been to a petting zoo before. Her mother never had the time or patience, and none of her foster families had ever thought of an outing like that. While she would never admit it to the others, she was looking forward to being able to pet a pig for the first time, or feed goats from her hand.

They stepped up to the small ticket booth and Alyssa bit her lip nervously as she looked at the prices. It wasn't expensive, the admission not nearly enough to cover the cost of such a place, but it was still going to eat up her weekly spending allotment and her jeans had started feeling a bit tight in the last week.

As her hand slipped into her pocket to get her wallet, Josh placed his hand briefly on her elbow. "I got this," he said, as he handed over two crisp twenty-dollar bills, enough to cover their costs as well as several bags of pellets to hand-feed the animals.

"Oh, you don't have to do that," Alyssa stammered out, torn between her desire to be free of owed favors and knowing she had limited funds.

He just gave her a smile and held out one of the brown paper bags filled with pellets. "I know I don't, but I want to. Here."

Her fingers closed on the bag as her lips curled into a smile. "Thanks." Optimism began to creep in as he held the door to the park open and motioned her to walk through.

Alyssa gasped as they entered the park, gleefully overwhelmed at the amount of animals and joy that filled the large space. Laughing at Brianna's squeal of happiness, she and Josh joined their friends at the gate to the goat pen and carefully slipped inside.

Immediately goats surrounded them, and Alyssa felt a pang of fear as the six goats closed in, encircling her and her friends. Then Josh laughed and knelt down to pet one, the creature pushing its furry head into his hand and tilting it sideways for a good ear scratching.

"Come on, Lyssa. Give it a try." He winked at her as he continued scratching the goat's head.

She took a deep breath, then bent over to pet the goat's back, surprised at the roughness of the fur beneath her fingers. A frustrated bleat filled the air, and she looked over to where a smaller goat stood at the fence, staring out at the passerbys.

"Hey, little goat, what's going on?" Alyssa murmured to the goat as she walked over, Josh a few steps behind her. The little goat melted under her fingers, turning its head left and right to move her fingers to the itches and pressing its warm body against her leg.

After dipping her hand into the bag of feed, Alyssa very carefully held a few pellets out to the small goat, placing them in her palm and keeping her fingertips out of the way, mimicking what Josh was doing next to her. The feel of the goat's whiskers on her palm tickled, and, before she knew it, giggles had consumed her body.

She spent several minutes just standing there, enjoying the freedom of the laughter as the goat finished the pellets and started nosing around her legs, searching for more.

"Sorry, little goat," she said amid chuckles. "I've got to save the rest for the other animals."

Their next stop was the large deer pen, and Alyssa stopped to stare at the fence for a full five minutes before her friends could convince her to step inside. She had only seen a live deer once, and only for ten lightning-fast seconds before the creature jumped in front of the car her keeper was driving.

Her body shuddered as she remembered the impact, the sudden, painful jolt on her body and the searing pain as her seatbelt burned its impression into her skin through her shirt. Her keeper had tried to avoid the deer, had swerved and slammed on his brakes, but it didn't help. Eyes wide open, Alyssa had seen the animal smash into the front of the car, the impact turning the rapid swerve into a sharp spin. It had flown up, shattering the windows on the driver's side of the car, and afterward she sat helpless on the side of the road, staring at the battered, jerking body, until the police arrived with the tow truck to take them home.

"Lyssa?" Josh's voice jolted her from the memory and the world around her spun in a rapid circle from the shift. Her fingers dug into the rough wooden fence in front of her, and she felt a warm hand on her shoulder steadying her as she swayed.

"I'm okay," she whispered, certain it was a lie and she would never be okay.

Josh's blue eyes came into focus as she blinked away tears. His hand slipped from her back and he leaned on his elbows next to her on the railing. "No, but you will be. We don't have to go in if you don't want to, Lyssa. There are other animals to see."

"No, it's okay." Alyssa took a deep breath and gave a reassuring smile to Brianna, who must have realized something was wrong and was heading toward them from her place among the deer. "I just didn't get a lot of sleep last night."

"Uh-huh." His tone was far from one of belief, but Alyssa sighed gratefully as he stepped away from the fence and toward the gate.

A grin split across his face as he held out his hand, "Ready to meet the deer?"

Her hand slid into his without a thought, and she felt part of her jagged edges smooth as she replied, "Let's do it."

Twenty-Seven

Sirens blared outside, pulling Alyssa away from the ceiling she was absently studying and sending Brianna scurrying to the window.

"Oh, what's that? What's happening?" Brianna bounced onto the bed beside Alyssa, pulling the curtains aside and watching the red and blue lights go flashing by. "Alli?"

Alyssa had curled herself into a ball on her bed, eyes clenched shut in fear that the sirens were coming for her. Her body jumped as she felt a hand touch her shoulder, and her eyes popped open to see Brianna sitting next to her.

"Alli, you're safe now. They're gone. They're not coming for you." Her friend gave her hand a brief squeeze before sliding off the bed to return to the pile of pictures next to her notebook.

"Yeah, I know. Sorry. I'm a little edgy today." Alyssa slowly uncoiled and stretched out on her belly, looking over Brianna's shoulders at the pictures on the floor. "Oh, who is that baby?"

"That's ... I don't know." Brianna flipped the card over to read the back. "Dawson, 1973. I guess it must be an uncle or someone. I've never heard of them, so I'm not going to stick them in."

Alyssa just grunted before she rolled over and returned to studying the ceiling. The day before her history teacher had given them a genealogy project to "emphasize the importance of the past upon the actions of the future". The assignment itself was simple, ask your parents for some pictures and information regarding your past, and make a family tree going back four generations.

Brianna had thrown herself into the project with full force, fascinated and aided by the close relationship she had with her family, complete with aunts and uncles, and four very alive grandparents. Alyssa was surprised that they had been working on the project for three hours now and Brianna had yet to notice that Alyssa's page for notes and sketches was still empty.

How am I supposed to do a family tree when I don't have a family? Alyssa thought glumly as she repressed a sigh. Her pencil scratched irritatingly as she wrote her name, then drew a single line upward, another line crossing that and leading to each parent. Overcome by a flash of anger and betrayal, she moved the lead point over the words, scratching out the entire thing in angry slashes and X's.

The image mocked her, acting like she had parents, a family, a history worth recording. She blinked back tears as she ripped the paper out of her notebook and tossed it into the trashcan. If she was going to have to do this project, she was going to do it her way. She wrote her name at the top in bright purple, curling the letters so that they looked like script. A clinical black line dropped down the length of the page, perfectly straight without needing a ruler.

Directly below her name in miniscule red letters, she wrote the names of her parents, one on each side of the line. In slightly bigger blue letters, she wrote her foster homes in corresponding order, each newer name lower on the page. The ones where she felt love, she added a small heart beside the name; the ones where she just felt like she was a small paycheck each month or just charity, she just left as text. *This is my family*, she thought with a touch of bitterness as she doodled between the names with flowers and vines, hearts and tear drops.

"That's beautiful."

A string of curses flew from Alyssa's lips as she jumped, startled out of her dark thoughts by her friend's quiet words. "Why do you and Caleb always insist on scaring me so freaking much?"

"Why do you insist on brooding and not paying attention to the world around you so much?" Brianna countered, one eyebrow raised and arms crossed in front of her chest. Her hand fell on Alyssa's as she went to rip off the sheet illustrating Alyssa's family. "No, you should turn that in."

Disbelief trickled through Alyssa at the thought of handing in the tree. "Yeah right. Mr. Sanders doesn't want crap like this. I'll just make another one with my mom and dad and say my grandparents both died before I was born or something."

"Alli," the constrained anger in Brianna's voice caused Alyssa to pause. "You aren't the only one with a screwed-up family, you know. I can't imagine what your life has been like, but I get not feeling loved or wanted, or feeling like you don't have a family to lean on. There are a lot of kids who feel the same way that you do, other kids still in the system, or kids who were adopted, or kids who have divorced parents. This assignment sucks for a lot of people, and maybe this will show the teacher how something as stupid as a family tree assignment can really hurt a kid."

Alyssa just sat there, speechless, as Brianna slid off the bed and went back to sorting through her pictures. "Bri, I never thought ... you're right. But I don't have any pictures to include. Do you think he'll mark it off?"

"You have those." Brianna pointed to the section of wall Alyssa had devoted to pictures, already hanging over fifty that Jessica had printed out for her.

She stared at them a moment, each picture bringing a joyful memory of her last few months with her friends. *How can it only have been a couple of months?* She thought as she slowly stood up and pulled some of the pictures down. "You guys are my family, after all. That's a great idea, Bri."

Brianna smirked. "Yeah, I have a couple. Just don't tell Caleb you are family, or you will never get rid of him!"

Twenty-Eight

"Romance, comedy, or action?" Josh's smooth voice asked through the phone Alyssa held to her ear with her shoulder.

"Um ... let's do comedy," she suggested as she carefully ran the nail polish brush over her toes. Spring had finally arrived with sunlight and warmth, and she was planning on wearing the new peep-toe shoes that Jessica had bought for tonight, Alyssa's first solo date.

"Sounds good to me. Want me to come pick you up in an hour and we can go from there?" She could hear his younger sister in background, shrieking at her twin brother. "Oh for fu - Ginny! Stop it! I'm sorry, Lyssa. I've got to go deal with this. I'll see you at six, okay?"

She chuckled as she hung up. A few days ago, Brianna had convinced her to stay after school and watch the boys' track team having their try-outs, so she saw the full force of Josh's family. He was the second child of the family, with an older sister who was in college, younger twin siblings who had just become teenagers, and his youngest sister who was in middle school.

Alyssa and Brianna sat in the stands, cheering on Josh as he sprinted down the track, gaining and keeping the lead throughout the one-mile trial race. His younger siblings screamed from the fence, jumping up and down at his clear win and telling everyone within earshot that they were related, while his older sister and parents just smiled.

Caleb slid onto the bleachers behind them and gave each of their ponytails a tweak. "I fail to see what is so fascinating about people running in circles."

Brianna just rolled her eyes. "Oh, puh-lease. You would be out here in a minute if the girls' team was here running."

He grinned. "That's different."

"Is not."

"Is so."

"Is not!"

Alyssa chuckled at their banter and leaned forward on the bleacher seat as the starting whistle blew for the second race. She watched as Josh shot from the starting line, his legs flying as they carried him to the first hurdle, calf muscles bulging as he sailed over the obstacle. As he finished he glanced her way, and Alyssa felt an odd fluttering in her stomach as he waved.

The look in Caleb's eyes as he glanced at her was one of amusement. "Huh, wouldn't have pegged that one for you. I'll have to let him know that if he breaks your heart, I'll break his-"

"Alli?" Jessica's voice drifted into the memory, bringing Alyssa back to the present, the nail polish brush still in her hand.

"I'm sorry, Jess. What was that? I was day-dreaming." She carefully capped the bottle and put it on her nightstand, tapping her heels on the carpet while her toes dried.

"I said, don't forget, I'll be out with Darren tonight, so call my cell if you need anything."

"Oh, okay." She looked at the woman and smiled as she took in Jessica's appearance. A dark blue, floral patterned dress hung to her curves, while the gold jewelry gleamed against Jessica's pale skin. Her black hair had been pulled up into an elegant bun, with curls escaping to cascade down her neck.

"You look really pretty, Jessica. What's the occasion?" Satisfied that her polish was dry and wouldn't smudge, Alyssa hopped up and started going through her clothes to get dressed for her own date.

Jessica blushed and fidgeted with her purse. "No occasion. It's just been a while since we've had time to talk about things or spend time together, so I thought I'd dress up a little bit more."

Alyssa's heart dipped, fully aware that she was aware that she was the reason Darren rarely came around. "He can come over, you know. The one ... incident ... on my record wasn't what it seems like, I mean, I never wanted ..." Her voice grew quiet as she added, "I promise I won't touch him."

For a moment, she wondered if Jessica even heard, then Alyssa found herself gathered in Jessica's arms, breathing in the scent of crushed roses.

"Is that what you have been thinking? Alli, never think I'm worried about that. Besides, he's an adult and you're just a kid. We've just been really busy is all. Don't you dare think it's your fault for a second."

After a moment, Alyssa pulled away and wiped the tear that had escaped from her eye. "Okay. Um, could you help me pick out an outfit? I have a date tonight and don't really know what to wear."

"A date? A real one? I thought you were just hanging out with a friend." Jessica gave her a stern look, then nearly squealed in delight and hugged Alyssa once again, lifting her off her feet. "Is it Josh? I like him. What are the plans?"

Alyssa plopped on the bed, all too ready to let Jessica dress her for the night. "Yes, a real one, and yes, it's with Josh. He's a senior at our school, and just moved into the area at the beginning of the year, so he kind of knows what I'm going through, being the new kid and all."

Jessica's head turned and she studied Alyssa for a long moment. "A senior, huh? And how do you know a senior?"

A blush crept onto Alyssa's cheeks and she picked up the hunter-green dress that landed in her lap. "He's a friend of Brianna's new boyfriend, Jeremy."

"The one from the petting zoo? You never told me how that went, by the way. I'm assuming it didn't go too badly?" The twinkle in her eyes offset the parental tone in her voice.

A smile lit up Alyssa's face as she remembered. "It was really great. We got to feed goats, and deer, and ducks. Then there was a place where we could pet donkeys and horses, and they had two little monkeys that they had rescued so we watched them playing in their enclosure and just laughed at them for a good half hour."

"And the boy?"

"He was a really good surprise. Josh was actually a lot nicer and more down to earth than I thought he would be since he's so popular. He never tried to make a move on me or anything. We talk a bit at school, but he's not overbearing, which is really nice. Even though I totally flaked out on him at one point, and thought he'd run away because I was acting crazy, he just took it all in stride and brought me back to earth."

"Sounds like a good catch. Go try that dress on." She nodded to the dress in Alyssa's hands and waited in the room while Alyssa slipped into the bathroom to try it on.

"That's so cute!" she said when Alyssa stepped back into the room.

Looking at her reflection, Alyssa found herself cautiously agreeing. The hunter-green dress was one that Jessica had bought years ago but never worn, and actually fit Alyssa perfectly. The halter-top style let her feel covered and comfortable, but had her shoulders and arms bare. The lower part of the dress was cinched at the waist, then flowed loosely, swaying and rippling as Alyssa turned to look at herself from all angles.

Loud beeping came from Jessica's purse, and she quickly fished out her cell phone and answered it. "Yep, be down in one second." Her hand gently cupped Alyssa's cheek and she gave her forehead a quick peck. "Have fun tonight. I should be home around eleven, so if you are going to be later than that, please, give me a call on my cell. And feel free to call me if you need me for anything, at any time. Okay?"

"Okay, Jess. Go on. Have fun." Alyssa sat at her vanity and surveyed the makeup choices that Brianna had given her after hearing about this date.

Jessica quickly darted from the room, then poked her head back in. "Oh, and Alyssa?"

"Yeah?"

"Let him know that if he touches you, he's toast."

Twenty-Nine

The lights in the theater dimmed around them, and Alyssa felt a moment of panic at the absolute darkness. Closing her eyes, she counted to five, then opened her eyes again when the movie screen began playing previews and advertisements, casting enough light into the theater to ease the fear.

"You okay?" Josh glanced her way, and she hoped the rise and fall of her chest and nervous jangling of her bracelet wouldn't give her away.

"Yup." She pasted a smile onto her face, then took a gulp of air at the strange look that met her eyes.

"You sure? It doesn't seem like it."

Alyssa took a deep breath and tapped her toe on the floor. "I will be. Don't worry about it. I'm fine."

There was no way she could tell him that this was the first time she had ever been in a movie theater. For some reason, she hadn't expected it to be so large, so dark, or so menacing. They had chosen a popular movie, and the theater was packed. The thought of so many people surrounding her brought a wave of anxiety and Alyssa felt her eyes tearing up.

"'Lyssa?" Josh gently tapped his finger against her hand where it clenched the shared arm rest in a white-knuckled grip. "We can leave if you want."

"No. I'm just ... a little claustrophobic I guess." She forced her hand to release its death grip on the armrest and took a deep breath as she clutched her purse in her lap.

His blue eyes stared at her a moment, then he grinned. "Here, switch seats with me." Josh stood up and stepped into the aisle, motioning for Alyssa to follow, then switching seats so that she sat in the chair next to the aisle.

She could feel her anxiety ease almost immediately, for while it was still dark and far too crowded, she now had an opening for escape. The movie started, and she became engrossed in the plot, quietly laughing at the antics of the characters and relaxing at the sound of Josh laughing beside her.

"I normally don't like this actor, but he's hilarious in this," Josh leaned over to whisper to Alyssa, his arm casually resting on the back of her seat.

Alyssa's body stiffened at the motion, but, when his arm stayed high enough to avoid touching her shoulders, slowly relaxed back. She remembered the day at the petting zoo, when he took her hand to guide her into the deer pen, and butterflies stirred in her stomach. Her hand moved to the arm rest, sharing the space with his, and she saw him give a tiny smile as the only acknowledgment of the slight touch.

"Want some popcorn?" He tilted the bag her way, and her fingers touched his as they pulled out a few kernels.

"Thanks," she whispered back, surprising herself with the easy feeling of touch. *It may only be a little one*, she bargained, *but maybe it means that one day I won't cringe every time someone breathes on me.*

~ * ~ * ~

The front door softly clicked shut as Alyssa entered the house and gave a sigh of happiness. For once, she felt comfortable in the presence of a male; *at least*, she said to herself, *someone other than Caleb*. Josh hadn't tried to touch her the entire night, beyond the small brushes of their fingers while eating popcorn, or when his hand would hover at her back when he opened doors.

Things are finally going right, she thought excitedly as she shrugged out of her light jacket and hung it on the peg by the door. Friends, a pet, a potential boyfriend, it was all surreal and she allowed herself one moment to ride the wave of bliss without letting the doubt creep in.

When she reached the door to her bedroom, she heard Jessica's voice and halted.

"I know it's a change, but she's family now. You can stay here without getting in trouble, you know. Once we get married, she's going to be living with us, so it would ease the transition."

Jessica's bedroom door opened and Alyssa quickly ducked into her room, briefly meeting Darren's eyes as he stepped into the hallway.

She quietly but rapidly shut the door, changing into her pajamas and taking off her make-up before cracking the door open again and peeking into the hallway.

Jessica stood at the closed front door, forehead pressed against it and shoulders slumped. After fighting a quick internal battle of doubt, Alyssa stepped out of her room and went over to her keeper.

"Jess, are you okay?" She pretended not to see Jessica quickly wipe her eyes.

"Yeah, just tired. Are you okay if I just go to bed and we talk about your date tomorrow?" Jessica smiled, though Alyssa knew it was forced, since it looked exactly like when she smiled when she was really crying on the inside.

"Yep. I was just going to get some water and then pass out myself. See you tomorrow."

Thirty

"Dreams," Mrs. Callen said as her purple whiteboard marker underlined the word with a flourish. "Today we are going to write about them. Your dreams, your hopes, your potential futures. Without dreams, we have no hope, and without hope, well, that would be an existence that is too horrible to even contemplate. The tiniest of seeds have hopes, hopes that the sun will come and the rain will give them nourishment, hopes that they will grow big and tall, spreading their leaves to the great sky above."

Beside Alyssa, Caleb rolled his eyes as he continued drawing a detailed human skull on his notebook. She giggled, both at his reaction and as a defense mechanism for the chasm she knew she was about to fall into.

"Oh good, we have a volunteer," Mrs. Callen pointed her pen at Alyssa. "Ms. Doe, what are some of your dreams?"

To live in one place for longer than six months, to know that I won't be living in a shelter in two years, to have two parents who love me. "To go to a good college," she said out loud, shoving the other, impossible, dreams back into the hole of her heart where they were kept safe.

"No, no. We need to go bigger! What about after college? What do you want to do with your life? Where will your life's journey take you?"

The intensely awkward silence was broken by Caleb's snort. "Far from this crap-hole, that's for sure!"

"Why, Mr. Rose, thank you for volunteering to answer the question. What are your dreams?" Mrs. Callen didn't even look upset, she was so accustomed to his attitude.

"Yeah, I don't think those are appropriate for school." His grin was cocky but Alyssa saw the way his shoulders slightly hunched and his foot tapped nervously.

Truth be told, she had no idea what she wanted to do with her life. Before her latest placement with Jessica, she had only been focused on surviving, on getting good grades, being on her best behavior, not getting kicked out of her current house. There was no future in her plan, no hopes or aspirations, only getting through today.

She stared at the blank paper in front of her and tapped her pencil, leaving a tiny trail of black dots. *What do I want to do with my future? Graduate high school, go to college, not be homeless, not be pregnant without a husband who loves me, survive.* She couldn't even think of what profession she would want after college. Any job that would take a chance on a girl with no permanent address, work history, or family references, would be fine by her.

My Hopes, she wrote at the top of the paper. *I hope I can keep my cell phone when Jessica gets married and realizes I'm not supposed to be part of her future plan. I hope I can stay in one place long enough to graduate high school. I hope Josh asks me on another date. I hope that Jessica keeps my cat safe when Darren convinces her to get rid of me. I hope my mother comes back and says she made a huge mistake in leaving and wants to be a family again.*

The last thought shocked her, sucking the breath from her body and causing a tear to fall before she could stop it. She angrily drew a line through it, pressing so hard on the paper that it tore and her pencil ran onto the desk below.

The paper suddenly was whisked off her desk and she looked up to see it pinched between Caleb's fingers. "Give that back," she hissed, glancing frantically between him and the teacher, who was busy erasing the board for the next segment.

He did, but not before his eyes skimmed the paper, and she saw his expression darken as he read through her secret hopes.

The bell rang and she jumped from her seat, making it two steps before Caleb's hand on her new backpack held her back. "Caleb, let me go."

"You don't really want that, do you? Your mother to come back?" His voice was equal parts concern and utter disbelief, and Alyssa slowed her pace to match his as they stepped in the hallway, held back by his insistent tug on her backpack.

Brianna joined them and shot him a glare. "Caleb, shut up."

"No, I want to know. Why would you want your mother to come back after all the crap she's put you through? You're better off without her."

"Because she's still my mom," Alyssa shot back as she turned the dial on her locker. "Maybe when she gave me up she was just really stressed, and now she's older and wiser and realizes her mistakes. Maybe she was in danger and left me to protect me, and when she's safe she'll come back and we'll be a family again. Maybe she did get rid of me, but we could start over, and I could stop having a new place to live all the freaking time."

"Alyssa, you don't really believe - oof," his incredulous response was cut off by Brianna's elbow sinking into his stomach.

"I have to believe it," she choked out, staring at the tiles of the ceiling to blink back her eyes. "My only other option is to believe that she left me on purpose, and I can't do that. I just can't. Mothers don't leave their children. It was just a mistake. She's going to come back for me. I know it."

Brianna cleared her throat and looked behind Alyssa, causing Alyssa to whirl around and find herself staring into Josh's face.

"Hey, Lyssa, you okay?" His hands reached out as if to touch her, but he drew them back before they reached her arm.

"I'm fine. I have been fine. I will always be fine. I. Am. Fine. Would everyone please stop asking me that question?" She grabbed her book from her locker and swung the door shut, the dramatic bang immediately drowned by the din of the hallway. "I need to get to class."

Caleb stepped beside her, his eyes meeting Josh's above Alyssa's head in a silent challenge. "Alright, let's go. Our financial futures await."

She looked up from her position between the two males and let out a huff of annoyance at the posturing. "Oh for the love of ... Would you two stop?"

Josh dropped the stare first, but he smiled as he gently took a section of hair that had escaped Alyssa's pony tail and tucked it behind her ear. "Sorry. Do you want to do something on Saturday?"

"Sure." She gave a little smile, suddenly self-conscious of the faded shirt she had chosen to wear that day and her behavior from earlier.

"See you then. Bye, Bri. Caleb." He nodded at her friends before walking back down the hallway.

Brianna squealed and jumped on Alyssa as she hugged her. "Another official date! That's so awesome."

"Ugh, girls." Caleb rolled his eyes and nudged them away from the lockers, herding them toward class. "Come on. You can write notes about McDreamy all you want and exchange them in study hall."

Thirty-One

If you could be any animal, what would it be?

Josh's text made her laugh and she rolled over on her stomach, laying her head sideways on her pillow.

A zebra

Me too!

She typed in **Liar** and giggled, feeling giddy from the hug they shared after the final bell of school that day.

Caught me. I'd be a tiger.

Rowr

Rowr back

Alyssa put down the phone, giggling as she grabbed her notebook for her finance class and looked over her notes for the day. They had spent the class discussing student loans, and she wanted to make sure that she understood the process so that she could go to college in two years. Loans and scholarships would be her only chance at paying for college, and she had to make sure that she had enough to cover room and board along with tuition.

The doorbell rang, pulling her from her studies momentarily as Jessica yelled, "I've got it," from her position in the kitchen.

"Hi, Jess. Long time no see."

Her breath froze in her chest as Alyssa recognized the voice deep in her core, memorized as a child and memorialized for six long years. She lay on the bed, paralyzed into silence, as a lifetime of emotions flooded her in an instant.

"What are you doing here?" Jessica sounded angry, her voice quiet, so quiet that Alyssa could barely make out the words as she jumped from her bed.

"Well, that's no way to greet me! I was in the area with Tim and wanted to drop by to introduce you to my daughter, Lizzy."

Her body moved off the bed on its own, then abruptly stopped as if her feet had become cemented to the floor, so rapidly that Alyssa stumbled, her hard fall silenced by the plush carpet below. *Her daughter?* She shook her head as she kneeled on the floor, fingers sinking into the carpet.

"How dare you come here! Do you ... have any idea ... done with us ..." Jessica's voice faded in and out as Alyssa pushed back the stars from her eyes and focused on her breathing.

She peeked out, seeing a woman standing in the doorway with perfectly dyed blonde hair, impeccably applied make-up, and a six-month-old infant dressed in a frilly pink dress held lovingly in her arms.

" ... thought you would be excited to see me ... been gone a long time ... realized family ..."

Alyssa gulped a breath. Why was Jessica so mad? Her mother came for her, finally, after all this time. Sure she looked different, and there was another child involved, but she still came. They could work that part out, she could adjust. Now Jessica would be free to continue her life with Darren and be done with her.

" ... I got my life together, Jess. A stable man, a house, it's finally coming together." Her mother sounded happy, and Alyssa realized she had never heard her mother sound happy.

"And what about Alyssa? Where does she fit into this plan?"

"Alyssa?" Her mother sounded confused.

"Your oldest daughter," Jessica spat out the words, "the one you left at school six years ago."

Hands clenched into fists, Alyssa waited for the answer, waited for her mother to ask about her, then she could go running out to hug for the first time since she could remember.

"That was a different life. I didn't want a child back then. Lizzy is my only daughter now. That child was a mistake. I should have just gotten rid of her when I found out I was pregnant and saved us both a lot of grief."

The carpet dipped and rolled below, and Alyssa felt the wave of nausea sweep through her body. *I must have heard her wrong, please, let me have heard her wrong.* Her back scraped against the doorjamb as she pushed back against the wall.

"Get out of my house," Jessica demanded, and Alyssa silently pleaded with her to bring her mother back to her room; surely her mother just misspoke. She shook her head, catching snippets of conversation as a slow, relentless pounding on her temples began to overwhelm her.

"Just a mistake ... signed over my rights with the court years ago ... Tim wouldn't want another kid anyway ... why so angry ... not your problem ..."

She banged her hands over her ears, willing the words to stop, willing them to change, feeling as though her heart was going to burst into shards.

"I never loved her like I do Lizzy, or like when George was born. She wasn't supposed to be mine, so I let her go so she could find somewhere better."

Her breath came fast and stars began to cloud her vision. She knew she had to get out, get away, before she heard more words that destroyed her biggest dream. Alyssa dragged herself to the window, sliding it open before pushing out the screen. She always found a way out of the house, and the tree outside her window provided an easy way to swing from her window to the ground below.

She landed on the grass, bare feet squishing on the ground below, soaking wet with the rain that poured down, drenching her and dripping from her eyelashes. It was the dark side of twilight, and the rain clouds had already cloaked the world in darkness. Her eyes stared for a moment at the black Mercedes parked in front of her keeper's house, the light from the front step illuminating the leather interior and two car seats safely secured in the back.

Backing away, she turned and ran, bare feet slapping against the sidewalk and impervious to the pebbles, twigs, and debris that lay below. She saw goosebumps on her arms, but her body felt numb as she ran.

Never loved her, not your problem, never loved her, not your problem. The phrase repeated in her head, hammered in with every step she took. After several blocks cramps seized her legs, slowing her pace to a stumble and her lungs burning in the cold air. Exhausted, Alyssa hugged her arms around a tree and cried, her tears hot against her cheeks as they mingled with the chilly rain drops and fell onto the rough bark.

"Lyssa? Alyssa!" Josh's voice carried through the rain that pounded upon the early spring leaves above her head. His arms brought warmth, and she couldn't dredge up the will to resist as he picked her up and carried her to his car.

The leather seat was slippery under her cotton yoga pants, and she felt a stab of guilt as she realized she was dripping water into the nice interior of the car. Just as she was about to slide out, Josh was in the driver's seat and locking the doors.

"Alyssa, what happened? Are you hurt?" He took her hand in his, using the other to brush her soaked hair from where it stuck to her face.

"She never loved me," Alyssa hiccuped out, eyes clenched shut and body curled into fetal position on the seat. "She said she never loved me. Never ever.

Never even wanted me. She loves them, but never loved me." She buried her face in her hands.

"Who?" Josh's voice rose in concern as Alyssa shook her head violently in answer. "Alyssa, who never loved you?" His hand withdrew, and she heard the car shift into drive, then felt it move forward. "Alyssa, I'm going to take you home."

"No!" she cried as her eyes popped open. "No, please no. Not there, not now."

"Did Jessica upset you like this?"

"No."

"Was it something one of your friends said?"

"No."

"Alyssa ..."

"You won't understand. She said I was a mistake. That she should have just ..." Alyssa's voice burbled into a strangled scream. "She said ... she said ..." the words caught in her throat as she collapsed into sobs once again.

He didn't reply, but she felt his hand on hers again, tentative and uncertain. Alyssa's fingers curled, grasping his hand in a death grip, holding on against the grief of the shattered dream of her mother's grand return.

The car stopped, and she rested her forehead against the cold glass window, opening her eyes to watch the raindrops pour down. A figure in a dark hoodie and black pants approached, and she shuddered as Caleb opened the car door and pulled her out.

Josh hovered to the side as Caleb wrapped his arm around Alyssa's shoulders, effectively shutting her off from the rain and the world as she breathed in the soothing scent of aftershave and his favorite incense, sandlewood.

"Caleb, bro, I didn't know where else to take her. I was heading to Jeremy's and saw her on the side of the road. She was just sitting under a tree in this downpour, sobbing. I can't make sense of what she's saying and she won't calm down. I know you can help her, please."

Alyssa felt Caleb's arm tighten around her body and his voice rumbled in his chest. "Alli, what happened?"

She shook her head, stumbling slightly as he took a step back, forcing her to face him.

"Alyssa Elizabeth Doe, I'm only going to ask one more time, what happened?" While his voice was terrifying, his gray eyes showed nothing but concern and love.

"My middle name's not Elizabeth," she stammered.

"I know, but it got your attention. Now, tell me what's going on."

"She said she never loved me, that I never should have been born. She left me, on purpose, intentionally, forever." The words came out in a whisper, barely audible through the rain, which increased into a deluge. "You were right. It was stupid, just a stupid, pointless dream."

"Alyssa. Who said she never loved you? Who left you?"

The rain abruptly stopped, and Alyssa sniffed, feeling as if she were ten-years-old again, standing in front of the school and staring at nothing but a long empty road.

"My mother."

Thirty-Two

The clock on her wall ticked, the sound grating against her ears, a metronome beating the seconds of her pathetic life away as Alyssa lay curled under her covers. *Unloved. Unwanted. Unloved. Unwanted.* The words pulsed in time with her heartbeat, refusing to release her from the pain seared into her soul seven days ago. Part of her wanted to demand answers, to scream until Jessica told her exactly how she knew her mother, call her mother and beg her to come back, but the other part, the more insistent part, didn't think her heart could bear more rejection.

She heard her bedroom door open and pulled herself deeper into the covers, the turquoise and violet cotton comforter hiding her from the world. Her ears picked up Jessica's sigh, and the mattress dipped slightly as her keeper sat on the edge of the bed. Alyssa swallowed hard, the motion an effort, her throat inflamed from crying and her eyes and nose raw

"Oh, sweetie. If I could take your pain, I would in a heartbeat. I hope you know that."

A gentle weight pressed against Alyssa's torso as Jessica bent over to kiss her forehead through the comforter. Alyssa shuddered, curling deeper into a ball and tucking her head under her pillow.

The door closed again, and silence filled the room, once again broken only by the ticking clock. She eased the covers off her head, the heat below stifling, and slowly blinked her eyes.

Why did I ever have you? Her mother's voice said the phrase over and over again, repeating for every time Alyssa heard it growing up. Every time she misbehaved, every time she couldn't finish her dinner, was sick, or asked for a new toy, the response would be, "Why did I ever have you?" But she never imagined her mother was serious until now, when she said the phrase after a speech about getting her life back together.

A furry face startled her as it filled her vision, amber eyes staring as the tiny voice meowed its displeasure at the lack of toys on her bed. Alyssa slowly stretched one of her hands out from under the cover, giving her kitten a small scratch under her chin. The effort was almost more than she could bear, her arm muscles sore from a week spent in bed, a week of refusing as much food and drink as she could until Jessica had threatened to take her to the hospital and hook her up to an IV.

"Your mom probably fought tooth and nail when they took you away, didn't she?" Her voice surprised her, gravely and dry, quiet, but booming against the silence of the room. The kitten meowed, pushing its way under the covers to rub her head against Alyssa's chin, whiskers tickling and bringing a slight smile to her face.

She rubbed her eyes again, wincing at the sunlight from the open curtains. A beautiful turquoise vase sat on her bedside table, filled with star-gazer lilies and Baby's Breath. Alyssa slowly emerged from the covers and picked up the small note that was attached to the vase.

Talked to Caleb today. Check your messages when you feel better. <3 Josh

A new round of tears sprang to her eyes. *He must think I'm a total nutjob*, she realized. *Heck, I think I'm a total nutjob.* Her phone rang, vibrating on the nightstand beside her, startling both her and the kitten.

The giggles started then, an automatic reaction to the kitten hissing at the phone, jumping straight into the air, and then unceremoniously sliding off the side of the bed. Alyssa wiped her eyes again and scooted herself into a seated position, propped up against her pillows.

Phone in hand, she scrolled through her message, including forty from Caleb, and sixty from Brianna. Finally she reached the latest from Josh and read it while holding her breath.

Lyssa, Caleb told me everything. Will you be at school this week? I miss you <3 Josh

Tears rolled down her cheeks as she clutched the phone to her chest, then typed a quick reply.

Yes. I'll be there tomorrow

Good. Meet at your locker

Feeling more optimistic, she swung her legs out of bed, padded across the hallway to the bathroom, and closed the door behind her. Just as she was getting ready to step into the shower she heard the doorbell ring, and another familiar voice grew louder as Patricia entered the house.

"Jessica, thank you for calling me. Is she packed?"

Alyssa's breath released in a hiss as she whispered, "No," and her hands pressed against the door. "No, please no. Not again. Please. I can't do this again."

"What? Of course not. Why would she be packed?" Jessica sounded genuinely confused. "Can I get you anything to drink? Coffee?"

"Coffee would be great." The couch creaked slightly, signaling that Patricia must have taken a seat. "Ms. Sona, I admit I'm a bit confused. Is your intention not to send Alyssa back to the agency for a better placement? That's typically the reason why a foster guardian calls us and asks for an immediate meeting. Since I was in the neighborhood, I dropped by instead of scheduling you at the office."

"No!" Jessica all but screamed, and Alyssa could picture her keeper in her head, pacing the floor and tugging on her hair the way she did when she was frustrated.

"No, Pat. Not at all. As I said on the phone, Alyssa felt the need to run away the other day, though she didn't go far, and I need to know where to go from here. No, not moving her or with punishment or
196

anything. I want to talk about how to help her feel secure again, after the blow of that woman showing up."

Alyssa let out a sigh of relief and crept away from the door, parting the shower curtain and stepping into the ceramic tub. The water was hot, instantly filling the room with steam and soothing her tight muscles as she stuck her head under the waterfall showerhead. Carefully, she drew in a deep breath as some of the emotional heartache eased.

She's still going to keep me, she thought, surprised at the amount of relief that filled her body, so strongly that she put a hand out to brace herself against the wall. She had never run away before, never acted out that severely in her entire time in the system. Part of her had been waiting for Patricia to show up, pack her belonging into a bag and escort her back to the agency, now with a run-away label on her file.

After a few more minutes she stepped out, wrapping herself in a towel to dart across the hallway.

"Alli? Is that you, hon? Can you come out here a minute?" Jessica called from the living room.

"Okay. One second," Alyssa called back, quickly pulling on a clean outfit and running a comb through her wet hair.

Patricia was leaning against the kitchen counter when Alyssa walked out, and the older woman gave a weak smile as Alyssa joined them. "Hey there, Alyssa. Jessica tells me you had quite a blow the other day."

She shrugged, not wanting to discuss the issue anymore, already erecting her walls.

"You missed school this week. I don't think you've missed more than two days in the years that I have been assigned to you."

"Yes, ma'am," Alyssa answered meekly. "I'm sorry. It won't happen again."

Jessica stepped over and draped an arm over Alyssa's shoulder protectively. "Hey, kiddo. You're not in trouble."

Patricia gave a nod and her tone immediately softened. "Why didn't you want to go to school, Alyssa? That's normally your safe place when things get tough at home."

"Because," she paused, contemplating the answer. Patricia was right. Usually school was her safe place, a place with rules that were fairly consistent across the country, a place where she could dive into the safety of math, science, and learning when her home life fluctuated so wildly. "Just, because, I guess."

"Fair enough. I won't push unless you are ready." Patricia gave Alyssa an encouraging smile, then nodded at Jessica before shaking her hand. "Call me if you need anything else."

The door softly clicked shut behind her and Jessica drew Alyssa onto the couch, lightly holding her hands. "Sweetie, you don't have to, but do you want to tell me why you didn't want to go to school last week?"

Tears brimmed in Alyssa's eyes as she gulped back the fear of trusting a keeper. "Because I have too much at school to lose. I couldn't stand to see Caleb, or Bri, or Josh, because I thought that you would be getting rid of me and it would hurt too much to know I needed to say goodbye."

"Oh, sweetheart." Jessica's arms were around her again, pulling Alyssa into a crushing hug. "I am never, ever going to get rid of you," she whispered fiercely into Alyssa's ear. "I know you've probably heard that before, but it's true. You are stuck with me for the rest of your life, like it or not."

"But, what about Darren?" Alyssa sniffed and stiffened at the obvious pain that flashed in Jessica's eyes at the mention of her fiancé. "He obviously doesn't like me since he's never here when I am. I don't think he's talked to me more than two times."

Jessica leaned back on the couch and stared at the ceiling. "It's not that he doesn't like you, he just needs a little more time to come around. Don't worry about him, okay? That's my job. To worry about him and you."

"Okay."

"You up for school tomorrow? Mr. Sanders was asking about you. He showed me your family tree and wanted my opinion. Alyssa, that was ... an incredibly creative and clever way to do that type of project, and I'm very proud of you."

"It was nothing." Embarrassed, Alyssa shrugged off the compliment. "And yeah, I'm going to go tomorrow. Josh asked me that too." A smile lit up her face as she thought of the flowers and his note.

"Mhm." Jessica smiled before kissing Alyssa's forehead. "You remember that feeling when bad things happen. There are a lot of people who love you, Alyssa, and we're all fighters."

Thirty-Three

"I look like a sausage. A giant green sausage." Brianna giggled as she looked in the dressing room mirror.

Coughing to hide the laughter, Alyssa shook her head in response. "More like ... asparagus."

"Oh gross! I don't want to look like asparagus! Get it off! Get it off!" Brianna bustled back into the changing room where Alyssa helped her with the zipper.

"What about this purple one?" The deep indigo dress was soft under Alyssa's fingers, and she felt a pang of jealousy that she would never own a dress like this one. After Brianna dropped her off at home , she was planning on visiting the local thrift shop, where she could hopefully find a dress for the spring dance that she could buy with her saved allowance.

"Nuh-uh, no way. That one is for you to try on." Brianna pushed it back toward Alyssa and turned to grab a candy-apple red dress from the hook in the room.

A sigh escaped Alyssa's lips before she could help it, and she glanced at the price tag once again, hoping futilely that it had changed. It had not. "Bri, you know I can't afford this. It's way too much."

"I knowww," she stretched out the word while grinning like a maniac. "That's why you aren't buying it, I am!"

"No, you're not," Alyssa protested. "Bri, it's too much. Your parents will kill you, and then me, and then you again."

"Wrong again. Why do you think I've been picking out the dresses I've been picking out? I've saved up three hundred bucks for this dance, and instead of blowing it on one dress for me, I thought it would be better on two dresses for us and agh!" Brianna ended her statement with a gurgle as Alyssa squeezed her tightly.

"You are the best friend ever!"

"I know," she replied with a wink. "Now, try on that dress. I bet that's the one that convinces Josh to finally kiss you! I can't believe he hasn't already. Gah, what a goober."

Alyssa slipped the dress on and turned around so Brianna could do the zipper. "It's my fault, really. There's been a couple times when I thought he might try, but then I get so anxious, and I'm sure I must look terrified so he backs off."

"Why are you anxious? You want him to kiss you, right?"

"Well, yeah, but -"

"And," she continued, "he wants to kiss you, right?"

"I guess so, Bri. But -"

"So what's the deal-ee-oh?"

"What's the ... what?

"Why haven't you two kissed? And how does this dress look on me?" Bri gave a little twirl in the dressing room to show off her latest choice.

"Wow, that looks amazing on you. And I don't know what I'm doing. With kissing, I mean."

Brianna stopped twirling and gave Alyssa a stare. "You mean to tell me, you have never been kissed by a boy before."

"No."

"Never?"

"No," Alyssa answered, but she felt her eye flicker and blood heat in fear as she remembered Jay. "Not ... no. Just no."

"Tell me," Brianna looked at her, and Alyssa knew she was seeing more than Alyssa wanted to reveal.

"It's nothing. I don't want to talk about it."

Brianna shrugged and slipped out of the dress, and they silently changed into their jeans and T-shirts to go purchase the clothes.

Once back in the bustle of mall walkways, Brianna linked her arm with Alyssa's. "Okay, let's just talk about Josh in general then. Out of all the boys in the world, why him? Not like I don't like him or anything! I'm just curious why him verses, oh, say, Caleb?"

Alyssa raised her eyebrow and maneuvered around a small toddler who had stopped in front of them to look at the tile floor. "I could ask you the same question. Why Jeremy instead of Caleb?"

"Ugh, why do I encourage you to give me as much crap as I give you? I just don't see Caleb that way. I love him to death and would go to the ends of the world for him, but romantically? It's just not there."

"Well, there's your answer. There are guys who are friends, and guys who are boyfriends, and he's the friend. Besides ..." Her voice trailed off and Alyssa felt her eyes grow misty.

"Besides?" her friend encouraged, noticing the pause and sheen in Alyssa's eyes.

"I don't have any great role-models who stayed in relationships when things get rough, and any of my ... experiences ... have been terrifying, and if I ever lost Caleb, I don't think I would survive. With Josh ... I mean, I really, really like him, and I hope that we have a long relationship, but if crap hits the fan, I know Caleb will keep me from doing anything stupid. If crap hit the fan with Caleb," she shrugged, "I'd be done for."

Brianna snorted. "Sure sucks for Caleb though, being surrounded by us hotties all the time."

Alyssa chuckled as she agreed, and took a deep breath as Brianna began humming, dropping the subject of boys and relationship and things that were destined to end in more heartache.

As they waited outside of the mall for Brianna's mother to pick them up, she turned to Alyssa and gave her a gentle nudge.

"One day I'm going to see under all those emotional layers you've built up, you know. Peel off each one like an onion until you aren't scared anymore, or ever feel like you are unloved."

"You don't want to do that," Alyssa murmured as she picked at her fingernails. "It will make you cry, just like peeling an onion. Sometimes it's better to leave things in their protective coating so you don't get hurt."

"That's okay." Bri gave Alyssa a little wink and linked their arms at the elbow. "I'm good at crying, so I might as well do a little on your behalf."

Thirty-Four

The class collectively held their breath as Mr. Bristow passed out their tests and Alyssa almost laughed as their expressions changed when each student received their scores. The spring dance was only two days away, and she knew most had parents who would not hesitate to cancel their child's plans if they wrecked their grade on this test, the biggest of the semester before the final exam.

"Caleb," Mr. Bristow paused just in front of Caleb's desk as he placed the paper down, "I'm not sure if I should be very proud of you, or very suspicious, but since you didn't obviously cheat, I'm going with proud. Good job."

Alyssa glanced at her own grade, a B+, before looking over at Caleb's and her mouth dropped. "An A? An A? How the crap did you get an A?"

"Must have been all that studying you did with me." He gave her a sheepish grin as he tucked the test into his book bag. "And not so loud. You're going to ruin my rep."

The bell rang and she slid her arm into his as they walked into the hallway. "No, really, how the heck did you get a better grade that I did if I was helping you?"

"Um, well ..."

She saw it then, the little glint in his eye that appeared when he was hiding something. "Caleb Rose! Tell me you didn't cheat!"

"No!" He bumped her gently with his hip. "See, I'm actually really good at this stuff. I have to be if I'm going to have my own construction business one day, I just hate doing the homework and since everyone already thinks I'm stupid, it's easier to run with it. Plus, you said you'd kick my as -, uh, rear if I don't graduate with you, so yeah."

Alyssa's relief at his honesty faded again to suspicion. "Then why did we do so much studying?"

"Promise not to get mad?" He waited until she nodded before continuing. "See, Bri told me that you were struggling with this section, and that it was above her head, but you didn't want Jess to know that you needed help, so I figured that if I studied with you, then you would get better at it too."

"I'm ... you're ... crap. You really are smarter than everyone thinks you are. We are so screwed." Alyssa gave his arm a squeeze before she saw Josh at her locker and ran up to give him a hug.

"Hey Lyssa, you having a good day?" He gave Caleb a nod hello and leaned against the locker beside Alyssa as she quickly grabbed what she needed for the next class.

"Yep. I passed my finance test so we are totally good to go this weekend."

He glanced nervously between Alyssa and Caleb. "Is Bri still coming? I'm really sorry about the whole Jeremy thing."

Alyssa bit her lip as Caleb answered, "I'm taking her instead." Jeremy had randomly broken up with Brianna two days before, and, though she was more angry and puzzled than sad at the development, she had begged Caleb to go to the dance with her so that she wouldn't be a dateless third-wheel.

"Awesome, man." He gave Caleb another nod and then kissed Alyssa on her temple. "Call you later. Have a good one."

"'K. Bye." She gave herself a minute to swoon as he walked away before the sound of Caleb's snort brought her back to reality. "Oh, stop. What's your problem with him anyway?"

His gray eyes stared until she began to squirm. "Simple math equation. You plus any guy equals overprotective me. The way I see it, you have no dad to protect you from the jerks of the world, so I get to take over that role."

"We've already gone over this. You're too young to be a dad." Alyssa poked a finger into his ribs to take the serious look off his face as they moved to their next classes.

"Oh good lord, girl. Whatever, big brother then, and you get all of the meddling, aggravating perks that go with it. Still want me as family now?"

A grin brightened her face as they parted in the hallway. "How the heck else am I going to pass finance?"

Thirty-Five

Black eyeliner and soft purple eye shadow brought out the sparkle in her eyes, and Alyssa stared at the mirror in awe of her reflection after Brianna had finished with her makeup. Not only did her eyes look prettier and brighter than ever before, but her skin looked flawless, and the light plum lip gloss Brianna had picked out perfectly accented the look without going overboard.

"Ms. Sona! We're ready for the hair now!" Brianna called out from Alyssa's room as she turned to the mirror and began to apply her own makeup.

"Oh goody!" Jessica giggled as she bounced into the room, curling iron and basket of hair products in her hands. "Come here, hon, and sit on the stool so I can work some magic with your hair."

Alyssa obediently sat and slowly began to relax as Jessica carefully ran a brush through Alyssa's long hair, effortlessly teasing out the snarls before separating the locks into sections and rolling each one in the curling iron.

She had never had her hair done before, and while Alyssa thought she should be terrified at the hot curling iron that was a mere centimeters from her head, she found it oddly comforting. A warm fuzziness filled her chest as she realized that this must be what trust was like, knowing that a person wouldn't hurt you, even if it would be so easy to do so accidently.

"Ms. Sona, that's beautiful! Where did you learn to do that?" Brianna gaped at the perfect curls that were gathered onto Alyssa's head before rippling down her back.

Jessica blushed, and Alyssa felt her fingers flutter on her neck as Jessica gathered the last bit of hair and pinned it in place. "My dream was to be a big stylist in Hollywood for all of the stars; at least, that was my dream when I was younger. I would sit with all of my dolls and do their hair, creating crazy hair-dos and elegant styles and everything in between. I actually was able to get a pretty good deal on tuition for a beauty school as well, even though I was just a sophomore in high school."

"Really?" Brianna was enthralled. "What happened? Why'd you go into banking?"

"My sister made some," she paused, "less than ideal choices when she was in high school that left the family reeling. So I picked the most important thing to me, my family and a stable future, and turned down the offer to dual-enroll in the college courses. By the time I graduated high school things with her had settled, but the ship had already sailed, so I went to college for finance instead."

"That's so sad." Brianna frowned into the mirror as she finished her make-up. "You gave up your life's dream because your sister screwed up. I hope she repaid you."

Jessica's face was full of conflicting emotions as she slightly turned toward Brianna, eyes sad but lips curved in a small smile. "In a way, yes, although it took a while for it to happen. Her biggest mistake turned into the best thing that ever happened to me."

Alyssa resisted the urge to twirl her hair, hoping to preserve the curls until Josh saw them. "But you gave up your future. What could she have possible given you to make up for that?"

Jessica gave a gentle squeeze to Alyssa's shoulders before standing up. "You never give up a future, you just step into a different one. I think it turned out to be a much better version of the future than I could have ever imagined. Want me to do your hair now, Bri?"

"Yes!"

Squirming like a puppy, Brianna jumped into place in front of Jessica, obediently holding out her hand to hold bobby pins, clips, and any other items Jessica might need during the process.

Alyssa watched them, Brianna's eyes closing and her face the model of contentment. Beneath Jessica's soothing fingers, Brianna melted, and Alyssa almost expected her to begin purring like a cat.

As if on cue, Tulip jumped onto Alyssa's lap, causing her to wince as the tiny claws dug into her leg. "You need a nail trim, Tulip baby."

She just looked up at her, blinked once, then jumped straight into the air, twisting her body and landing all fours. A blur of movement, and she was sitting on Jessica's lap, tiny paws feverishly swatting at Brianna's curls as they bounced with her laughter.

"No, no," Jessica admonished, voice firm even though her shoulder's shook, "that's not for you, little girl." After being gently placed on the floor, the kitten took off again, jumping high onto the wall for no apparent reason before careening out into the hallway.

Brianna's breath came out as a snort, then she fell into a fit of giggles so severe that Jessica accidentally jabbed her with a bobby pin. "I think her off button is broken!"

"I think it was never installed to begin with," Alyssa said under her breath. Many of her nights were sleepless now that the cat had firmly established her pillow as her sleeping place, and she would frequently wake up in the middle of the night to find her curled up on her chest or neck. Which was fine when they got her a month ago, but was now making it difficult to breathe.

"So, Brianna," Jessica said as she added a few rhinestone studded hair clips to Brianna's updo. "Are you excited to have Caleb as a date tonight?"

A grin split her face. "Ooooh, yeah." She whipped her phone out and turned on the camera feature. "I am getting so many blackmail pictures tonight of him in his penguin suit. Hopefully. Oh crap, what if he actually wears the tuxedo T-shirt that he was talking about? He would totally do something like that."

"Yeah, he would," agreed Jessica and Alyssa simultaneously before bursting into giggles.

"How about you?" Jessica turned to Alyssa as she tucked the last strand of Brianna's hair into place.

"Are you excited about your first big dance with Josh?"

"Um, um," Alyssa stammered, speechless as her cheeks began to flush.

"That means yes," Brianna translated.

Chuckling as she stood, Jessica helped both girls to their feet so they could finish getting dressed. "Just don't make him work too hard to kiss you, okay? You've got to hold on to the good ones with everything you've got."

Thirty-Six

It doesn't get any better than this, Alyssa thought as she swayed to the music, wrapped up in Josh's arms and dancing beneath the stars. He had sensed her beginning to feel a little too surrounded in the crowded gym, and led her outside to the small patio where the seniors hung out during their lunches and study halls.

Alyssa smiled and sighed in contentment as she rested her head on Josh's shoulder and looked at the beauty surrounding them. The dance committee had gone above and beyond for this dance, draping sparkling lights on the posts around the patio to form a dazzling curtain, and creating beautiful flower and sea-glass centerpieces for the tables laden with snacks and drinks.

Inside, they had gone even crazier, covering the gymnasium walls with lights, streamers, and beautiful big glittering stars. The students had even created a net that extended across the ceiling of the gym and filled it with hundreds of blue and white balloons. White pillars carved of Styrofoam stood in front of the bleachers, giving the room the aura of a sunken Greek city instead of a stinky high school gym, and the tulle drapery further hid the bleachers and cinderblock walls from sight.

She had never been to a dance before, and was shocked to see a real DJ, complete with pumping music and a fantastic light show as they entered. Alyssa felt her cheeks flush when she remembered her friends' reaction to her astonishment, and the way Josh quietly looked at her when she admitted she had never been to a dance before.

"Lyssa?"

His soft voice compelled her to look up, and Alyssa nervously pushed a curl from where it had fallen onto her forehead. "Yes?"

"I'm sorry for Brianna's sake, but I'm really glad that her dating Jeremy meant that I was able to meet you."

"Me too. It's kind of crazy to think that we've only known each other for like, two months or something, and you'll be leaving for college soon." *Oh crap, why did I say that*? Alyssa admonished herself. *It's not like I'm his girlfriend and should care.*

"Yeah, but we still have a lot of time before that happens, and I want to show you the world while I can. Alyssa, I was wondering, I mean, it's just that, um." He paused and swallowed, moving a hand to run it through his hair before gently placing it onto Alyssa's back.

"Um?" Alyssa lightly teased, nervous at his sudden loss of composure.

Then he looked down at her with such intensity that she felt her legs shiver, and she licked her lips, tasting the cherry lip gloss she had applied in the bathroom before they came to the patio.

"Lyssa, I have really loved spending this time with you, and want to spend as much time together as we can before the end of the summer. But, I don't want to spend it as just friends, so I guess what I'm asking is, will you be my official girlfriend?"

"Uh-huh," Alyssa answered, spellbound by the glittering lights around her and the butterflies doing dips and swirls in her stomach. She blushed as she realized what she said and fidgeted with the collar of his shirt, smoothing it down with her fingers.

"I mean, I'd love to be your girlfriend," she answered, relieved that this time she was able to get out more than just "uh-huh."

"Oh good," he laughed nervously, just before he slightly leaned down and kissed her.

It was everything she had imagined, her heart soaring and stomach fluttering as his lips touched hers, and his arms gently pulled her closer. *Thank you, world, for this little moment*, she thought in a silent benediction, losing herself in the thrill of being with someone and not feeling afraid.

Applause broke out behind them, and Alyssa felt her cheeks heat as Josh pulled away with a smile. She smiled back at him, "My friends?" she asked, looking into his eyes.

Josh just nodded, still smiling, and draped his arm over Alyssa's shoulder as she turned around to find Caleb and Brianna grinning maniacally at them.

"We couldn't resist," Brianna said, jumping up and down, her heels clicking on the cement of the patio. Alyssa grinned back as Brianna scooped her in for a hug and whispered, "He's so perfect for you," softly into her ear.

Caleb just gave his half-smile, then held out his hand to Josh. "Welcome to the family, man. Just know that if you make Alyssa cry, I make you cry."

While the comment had Alyssa sputtering with indignation, Josh simply laughed and took it in stride, pulling her close to his side before answering. "If I ever make her cry, you have full permission to knock some sense back into me."

"Come on," Alyssa said, feeling a little too much attention, "let's go back inside and enjoy the night."

Thirty-Seven

Though it was well past midnight by the time Alyssa arrived home, the front door was unlocked and she entered cautiously, waving Josh away when she heard Jessica and Darren's voice drifting from her keeper's bedroom. After quietly turning the deadbolt in the door, she removed her heels and tip-toed back to her room, wanting to give them some privacy since she knew Darren would leave the second that he knew she was home.

Alyssa smiled as she unzipped her dress and let it fall to the floor, quickly stepping into her soft cotton pajama bottoms and tank top before hanging it on the back of the door. Even her questions about Darren's behavior couldn't spoil this night. She had a boyfriend, for the first time ever, and real friends, and it was starting to look like she might have found a permanent keeper with Jessica. For once, things were looking up.

She let herself flop back onto the bed and felt as if her cheeks were going to fall off from grinning. He had kissed her, a real kiss, and it had been wonderful. Eyes closed, she let her mind drift over the events of the night, too wired to sleep but not wanting to go

217

shower until the adults fell asleep and she knew she would not be a bother.

Jessica's door slamming shot Alyssa up in the bed, and she slid off the side into a defensive crouch as angry voices filled the hallway.

"Darren, don't leave. Let's talk about this when we aren't both stressed and exhausted. I don't want you driving when you're this upset," Jessica's voice pleaded.

His was angry, rough and louder than Alyssa had ever heard. "Discuss what, Jessica? Everything has already been said. You already made the decision for us. You said this was a temporary thing, helping a teen get back on her feet. Now you are telling me this is permanent? What the hell, Jess?"

Now Jessica sounded pissed. "No, you heard what you wanted to hear. It was never temporary to me. Taking care of a child isn't temporary. It's a lifetime commitment and one that we talked about, in length, when I found the agency that had her and started the process. It's not my fault you didn't take me seriously."

"Of course I didn't take you seriously, Jess! Who in their right mind takes a freaking sixteen-year-old into the house for good when they are in their twenties?"

Alyssa sank onto the floor by the bed and hugged her knees tightly, the joy of the night spiraling into a compact little seed of hope that she frantically clutched in her chest.

"I do!" Jessica screamed back. "A lot of people do, Darren. What's so crazy about it? There's a little girl who needs help, and we are in a position to help her. It's not that difficult of a concept."

"What's so crazy? Are you serious? We're supposed to put our whole freaking life on hold for some slut's offspring?"

"Do not ever refer to Alyssa that way! None of this is her fault and this is the least I can do to make up for her having to bounce from house to house for six damn years because my damn parents didn't have the heart to try to fix Ashley's mistake."

"Oh, sure, now you care. Why is it that this came up nine months ago, huh? We've been together for three freaking years and you never once mentioned fixing your sister's mistake by wanting to foster a teenager, then we're engaged and BAM. Screw us getting married, or buying a house, or moving away from this podunk town to start a family. Is this your way of walking? Of calling off the wedding?"

"You know that's not it, and if you would calm down and let me talk ..."

"You aren't even getting any money for her, so why the hell are you throwing your life away for some brat?"

"Because she's my niece and family actually means something to me! I thought it meant something to you too."

Alyssa swayed with the statement, hearing the break in Jessica's voice as she shifted from anger to sadness and then steely resolve. Knees curled to her chest, she hugged herself, physically pulling herself together, confused and terrified.

"Jess."

"She's my family, Darren. And if you can't live with that, well, then I'm sorry but that's the way it's going to be. But ever since I found out about Ashley abandoning her, I have spent every moment I am away from you trying to find my niece, and then fighting to be able to get custody of her, so don't you dare pretend that this is just all on a whim."

"That may be, but I didn't agree to this, Jess. I didn't start this relationship with the intent to have a teenage kid in my care when I'm only twenty-six. I love you, but I can't do that, so if you really intend on keeping her, then you are saying goodbye to me."

"Then goodbye, Darren. I love you, but I'm not screwing her over like everyone else in my family already has."

Now, Darren sounded scared. "Jess, honey, don't do this. You know I need you."

"No," Jessica's voice broke, scaring Alyssa. "No, you want me, and maybe right now you need me, but you'll be okay in the long run. You'll move on and find someone new. Alyssa won't, can't. I'm sorry, Darren, but she and I are a joint package now, and if you need to walk away, I understand."

"Fine, if that's the way it has to be, then just ... fine."

Alyssa cringed as she heard him cursing at the front door, which she had locked on her way in. Tires squealed as he pulled out, and then a heavy silence fell over the house.

~ * ~ * ~

Several hours later, the sounds of quiet sobs pulled Alyssa gently from her sleep, and, as she looked around the dark room, she realized they were coming from the living room. Wrapped in a thick bathrobe, she padded to the door, cringing as it creaked loudly, despite her attempt to quietly check the hallway.

"Alli? Is that you?" Jessica called from the living room.

"It's just me. I thought ... I heard ..." She hovered in the hallway, unsure if her presence would be welcomed or an intrusion.

Red-eyed and puffy-cheeked, Jessica tried to give a comforting smile. "So that's why the door was locked. I'm sorry you had to hear that. I thought you were going to stay at Brianna's tonight."

"You said," Alyssa whispered, terrified as she crept closer to the couch, "you told him I was your niece. Am I really? Why didn't you tell me? Why did you tell me you didn't know where my mom was? I don't understand."

Jessica gave a sad smile and moved the pile of pictures and giant scrapbook from the couch to the table. "Up until a few weeks ago, I had no idea where your mom was, or what happened to you, since she broke off all communication with the family when she was pregnant. Alyssa, I wanted to tell you, but when I was finally able to get custody of you, your case worker suggested that it might be best for us to get to know each other first before throwing the complications of family into it."

"In case you didn't like me," Alyssa murmured dejectedly as she perched on the couch.

"No." Jessica gave a soft laugh as she wiped away the tears leaking from her eyes. "In case you didn't like me. Sometimes it can be harder going to family, because it's easier to remember what you lost. We also thought it would be better for us to get to know one another without you being angry at me for not taking you in sooner, because I am angry enough for both of us for that."

"Why weren't you able to?"

"Because I wasn't a good enough guardian for you yet," Jessica explained sadly. "I was nine when your mom got pregnant, still a kid myself. She cut off all contact with us after my parents kicked her out, so I never knew what she ended up doing. I didn't even know that anything had happened until I overheard our parents talking about you about a year ago. Then I had to go through the process, which was made even harder by my age. Most twenty-four-year olds can't support a family, so I had to make sure that I had a place to live that would accommodate both of us, a stable job, everything. By the time I did that, you had been moved so many times that it was impossible for me to find you, and the agency had an issue with their records ... it took forever."

"I didn't know, but Darren ..." Alyssa's eyes fell to the pictures and scrap book on the table, hundreds of pictures of Jessica and her fiancé, happy and carefree in exotic locations and pristine beaches. "You threw that all away."

"No, life presented me with a choice. Sometimes life gives you two things that you can turn into one future, sometimes it makes you pick one. In my version of the future, I could have both. Just because you are here doesn't mean I can't get married, or have another kid. If anything, it makes it better, because you can be my built-in babysitter."

"I am pretty good with kids," Alyssa admitted as Jessica gave a quiet chuckle.

"Darren didn't see the future that way. He and I both had choices that we could make, Alyssa. When we first started dating, he took a full-time position with the company that hired him as an intern that summer, and I made the choice to move out here with him. Now, it was up to him to make the choice to stay or go. I don't blame him for going, but me going anywhere without you was never an option."

"Oh," was all that Alyssa could reply, her head reeling from the despair of abandonment to elation that someone wanted her, fought for her. "I don't even know what to say."

"That's okay." Jessica wiped her tear-dampened hands on her jeans and stood up, pulling Alyssa with her. "It's been a long night. Let's get some sleep, and we'll talk more in the morning, okay?"

"Okay." Alyssa gave Jessica a tight hug before walking down the hallway. "Hey Jess," she softly called as Jessica went to shut her bedroom door, "thank you. For everything."

Thirty-Eight

The scent of woody, slightly musky incense greeted Alyssa as she stepped through the door of the tattoo parlor, hesitantly trailing behind Caleb, who walked confidently through the door. She immediately saw the source sitting on a tall counter in front of them, a beautifully sculpted ceramic incense holder shaped like a lotus flower.

"Why am I here again?" she quietly asked Caleb, who just gave her one of his twitch-grins as they approached the counter.

"Because I still haven't given up on convincing you to get one." He winked at her before turning to the heavily tattooed woman behind the counter with fire-engine red hair. "I have an appointment with Jake, last name is Rose."

The woman looked him up and down, shaking her head. "Can't ink under eighteen. It's the law."

"Well, it's a good thing I'm not under eighteen then." He gave a cocky grin as he handed over his ID, the date clearly stating he had turned eighteen the day before.

"Jake!" she called, and a lean man with arms covered in bright designs came out of the back room with a grin.

"Caleb! Welcome, welcome. Finally I can do this legally. Come sit down. I've got the pattern all drawn up so let me know if you want to make any tweaks." He gave Alyssa a onceover, and she immediately felt self-conscious in her faded jeans and pale green peasant shirt. "Your girlfriend getting one too? Half price."

"She's not my girlfriend," Caleb responded as Alyssa paled and shook her head vehemently at the suggestion. "More like the good angel who sits on my shoulder and keeps me from making too many stupid decisions."

"Ah, we can all use one of those, that's for sure. You're a lucky guy."

Alyssa's eyes wandered as they moved to the back section of the room, Jake motioning for her to take a seat on a spinning stool while Caleb slid into the leather chair and propped his bared arm on the rest.

It was a different atmosphere than she expected for a tattoo shop, neater, cleaner, though still with a slightly edgy vibe that was a cross between an off-beat coffee chop and an art gallery. Granted the only tattoos she had seen were done by amateurs with no problem taking under-age clientele and no license to show, but she still expected it to be seedier, grungier, and far less hygienic.

Instead, she saw a beautifully tiled stone floor that led to bright maroon walls, lit with multi-colored glass sconces on the walls as well as table lamps positioned at every station. Portraits of tattooed people hung in dark frames, and sections of the walls were painted in brightly colored hues, graffiti-styled names flowing into stunning and intricate designs. Her eyes fell onto the tattooed woman at the counter, who gave a small grin before motioning Alyssa over. She went, carefully closing the waist-high swinging door that allowed entrance from the waiting room to the stations.

"Not quite what you were expecting from a place called Inked Monkeys, is it?" Metal flashed in her mouth as she spoke, and Alyssa realized she was seeing a tongue piercing for the first time.

"Uh, no, not really. I'm not really sure what I was expecting though." Alyssa glanced over to where Jake sat next to Caleb, gloved hand moving the tattoo gun like a paintbrush, the tip of his tongue stuck out as he concentrated on the intricate shading.

"It's all about the vibe, sugar. Getting a tattoo should be exciting, fun, a little scary, but the last thing you want is to pick up some kind of disease. Jake worked hard to find a happy medium between edgy and fun, while keeping everything clean and unique. People come here from all over to find a tattoo that will express their personality, and from all walks of life."

Alyssa gestured to the paintings on the wall. "Are those all ones that Jake did? They're beautiful."

"Mostly, although a few were done by his mentor." She straightened up from her elbows and pushed off the counter, leading Alyssa back into the tattoo area and up to one painting. "This has always been my fav, done by the master himself."

"It's ... incredible." Alyssa felt her voice drop in awe as she stared up at the life-size oil painting. It was the view of a woman's back, bare of clothing and with her long black hair swept over her shoulder in one hand. A geisha adorned her skin, inked dress rippling in an imaginary breeze as cherry blossoms drifted through the air. Her dress was done in blues, greens, and reds, the colors so vivid and the details so precise that Alyssa imagined the geisha could step off the woman's back and into the tattoo parlor at any moment.

The woman smiled again, then gave Alyssa a look. "So many people think that tattoos have to be bad, offensive, controversial, but it's all art. Ink is such a beautiful way to adorn the human body, to turn the scars into emblems of honor and help heal the internal hurts with external beauty."

Her face turned from the painting, and Alyssa saw what she could only describe as bliss on the woman's face, the piercings and vivid makeup softened by the inner glow. A buzzer went off, signally the opening of the shop door, and the woman went to greet their newest client while Alyssa moved back to her seat by Caleb, curling up with her new favorite novel.

Over an hour later, she put her book down and stretched, back tight from being curled in the chair, though it was fairly comfortable. Alyssa blinked her eyes and rolled her shoulders, noticing that several other clients had entered the room and were seated in various positions at different stations.

"Does it hurt?" she asked, teasing Caleb with the question as his eyes were closed and his jaw twitched as if in pain.

"Feels like heaven," he responded through clenched teeth.

Jake chuckled, "No worries, man. Only a few more minutes and I'll be done with the naked chick."

"The what?" Caleb's eyes popped open and looked down at his arm in terror, his head flopping back when he saw there was no naked woman on his arm. "Don't do that to me, man. It took me forever to figure out what I wanted. I don't need you going all nuts on me."

"No worries." The buzzing of the gun ceased as Jake leaned back and rolled his shoulders. "Alright, that's it for now. I want you to come back in a few weeks to see if I need to touch up any of the lines, but you're good."

Caleb stood, stretching his back before walking over to the full length mirror and grinning at the new design adorning his arm. "Well done, my man. Well done."

"What is it?" Alyssa stepped next to Caleb, fingers tracing the design as they hovered over his skin.

"It's called a Rod of Asclepius, one of those Greek guys you always talk about. It's about healing, and strength. This snake crawling up the staff represents my demons, and this snake my protectors. They meet at the bottom of my wrist at the compass rose, a play on my name, and a reminder to stay the course, and keep going the right direction in life."

"I love it," she whispered, the words not nearly adequate to describe how the piece of art moved her, how it already seemed as if it had always been a part of his skin.

"It's a promise to myself, that I'm making partly because of you. You have fought so damn hard for everything, and always worked so hard to make yourself a better person, that I'm done throwing away my future just for the hell of it. From now on, no more screwing up my future; at least, not on purpose."

"Does that mean you'll be doing your homework on a regular basis?"

"Don't go all crazy, now. Let's start with tattoos."

Thirty-Nine

Alyssa glared at the setting July sun as she hurried up the front steps to her house and silently cursed the lack of lights within. She had hoped to get home before Jessica had to leave so she could tell her, in person, about her job offer to work as a teller at Jessica's bank. Now she was going to have to call Jessica to tell her, which seemed so unappreciative of the good word she put in for her, or wait until after Jessica got home from her hair appointment.

She took a moment to look at Jessica's home, her home for the last seven months. The six-month marker was a big one for Alyssa, and she felt a smile creep onto her face as she hopped up the front steps and checked the mailbox for anything important.

Alyssa stepped through the front door, and as the door clicked shut behind her, a deafening cry of "surprise" echoed through the living room and attached kitchen. Heart racing, Alyssa slammed her hand on the light switch, looking around the illuminated room, filled with her friends as well as Jessica and her caseworker, Patricia.

"Hi, sweetie. Happy birthday! You're seventeen today!" Jessica came over and took the purse from Alyssa's hands, pushing her gently into the room.

"I'm, I don't, what's, um. Hi?" The room burst into giggles and Brianna came bounding over from her place behind the couch to wrap Alyssa into a bear hug.

"Happy birthday, Alli. Jessica has been working for weeks on this party, and you have no idea how hard it was not to spill the beans." Brianna's eyes twinkled as she laughed.

"Thanks! I can't get over this. You guys are so bad at keeping secrets too! Give me a minute to process that you aren't trying to kill me."

Caleb chuckled and pointed at the streamers that draped across the ceiling. "You were with me when I bought those. We're not bad at keeping secrets, you're just bad at figuring them out."

"You said they were for your sister!"

"Yup. You, sister, sounds about right, don't you think?"

Tears filled her eyes as Alyssa wrapped her arms around his neck and he lifted her into the hug. "Thank you, Caleb. For everything."

Next she found herself wrapped in Josh's arms, his lips soft on her forehead. "Happy birthday, Lyssa."

"Thanks. I'm so happy that you made it back for this." She took in a deep breath of his cologne. He had only been away a week for his college orientation, but it felt like forever. Tears welled in her eyes as she thought of him being away for the next four years.

His finger brushed the tear away and his arms held her safely against his chest. "Hey, we'll make it work, and I'll be back during breaks. You'll have no problem getting a scholarship and can join me when you graduate. This is just the beginning for both of us, okay? Now enjoy your day."

"Presents! Presents! Presents!" Brianna's voice was the loudest as she led the chant, causing Alyssa to blush as she pulled away from Josh and he led her by the hand to the table of presents.

"The blue one is from me," Brianna pointed as she bounced up and down on her toes. "Open, open, open."

Alyssa laughed as she picked up the bright blue package and carefully tore open the wrapping. Her jaw dropped as she saw the box for the newest touchscreen tablet and she looked in disbelief at Brianna. "Tell me this is just the box and there's really just a paperback novel or something in here."

"Nope! It's all there, Alli. My parents helped a little."

"Thank you, thank you, thank you, thank you!" Alyssa ran over and hugged her friend.

"Now you can take your books wherever you go, and have an easier way to talk to Josh once he leaves for college."

"I can't even ... I'm ... thank you."

Josh held out a long, rectangular box. "This one is from me. I really hope you like. I'm still figuring out this whole, girlfriend gift, thing."

She chuckled as she opened the paper and saw a black velvet box. Inside lay a bracelet, the silver chain covered in charms and sparkling under the lights. Her fingers lightly brushed each charm, a book for her love of reading, a horseshoe for luck, an angel wing for faith, and a heart for love. Above the bracelet nestled two earrings, silver roses studded with bright red rubies, her birth stone.

"Josh, I'm speechless."

"Good." He gave her a chaste kiss as she wrapped her arms around his neck. "I wanted you to have something to remind you that I'm here for you, even if I'm physically not here."

Alyssa turned as Patricia gave a small cough, smiled, and held out an envelope. "It's not much, not nearly enough, but I thought you deserved a little something special on your birthday since so many went unnoticed. Open it up."

Alyssa carefully opened the envelope, eyes misting as she opened the envelope and saw a photo of her and four-year-old Drew playing catch. "How did ..."

"It was mailed to the agency last week. I thought you would want to have it. You did good, kid."

She flipped over the picture, then wiped a tear from her cheek as she read the note on the back.

Alyssa, I'm so sorry we couldn't be your forever home. Wherever this finds you, I pray that you are well, and know how blessed we were to have you in our lives – Theresa, Nathan, and Drew

"Thank you," she squeaked, overcome with emotion and unable to rise from her seat on the couch between Jessica and Brianna.

Jessica handed her another present, wrapped in Mickey Mouse paper. "Sorry," she blushed as Alyssa gave her a look of disbelief, "time got away from me and my boss had that at work from her kid's birthday."

The wrapping paper fell to the floor, revealing a beautiful leather envelope, the type that held diplomas or important paperwork.

"What's ..." Alyssa's voice cut short as her hand flew to her mouth and her vision blurred with tears. "Oh, Jessica, you really did it, I mean, it actually, it's ..."

She stared at the certificate of adoption that sat protected in the leather envelope. No longer was she Alyssa Doe, the unwanted child of Ashley and Jack Doe. Now she was officially Alyssa Sona, forever tied to Jessica Sona.

I have a family, she thought as her heart swelled with love. That piece of paper, the name change, such basic things that she had wanted for so long, were real and tangible in her hand.

"This one next. It's my idea and design, but everyone chipped in." Caleb handed her a large, bright green package.

Alyssa unwrapped it, still wiping tears from her eyes, and started laughing as she opened the box only to find it holding an even smaller box, and that one a smaller box. She opened the smallest box and pulled out a pendant that hung on a delicate metal chain.

It was a compass, a perfect circle of silver surrounding a pale gold tree of life. The cardinal directions glittered with tiny diamonds, a bright green emerald indicating north.

"Now you can always find your way home, no matter where life takes you," Caleb whispered, as everyone gathered around her.

As she stood still, lifting her hair to the side so that Jessica could place the necklace around her neck and clasp the tiny closure, Alyssa finally believed it to be true.

The Reality of Foster Care

While sad, Alyssa's story is far from fantasy. According to the U.S. Department of Health and Human Services, Administration for Children and Families, in 2012 there were nearly 400,000 children in foster care at any given time, with the average age of the child being nine-years-old. Some of these children will be returned to their homes, some adopted, and others will remain in the foster care system until they "age-out" around the age of 18.

Nearly half of these children have chronic medical problems and, if under the age of five, developmental delays. Up to 80 percent have very serious emotional problems, which can be expressed in a multitude of ways, everything from anger and outward destruction, to depression and self-harm.

Alyssa's fear of "aging-out" is a very real one. Per the 2012 report, only 2 percent of eligible 16-year-olds were adopted, and 1 percent of eligible 17-year-olds. Studies have shown that foster children who age-out of the system are more likely as adults to experience unemployment, incarceration, homelessness, and have untreated medical conditions.

How can we turn this around? That is a very complicated question, but it starts with knowledge. Learn about the foster system, and, if you feel compelled, takes steps toward becoming a foster parent, respite care-giver, or center volunteer. Know that these children are out there, and be aware of situations that will put them onto destructive pathways, whether it be emotional or physical. If you cannot give your time, many foster care centers will gladly take monetary donations which will provide the children in their care with new clothes, backpacks, school supplies, or hygienic supplies.

If you are a foster child, find help and work toward a better future. The way is going to be difficult, but you can overcome the odds and rise above everything that has happened to you. Find support groups, search out where you can find aid, and never give up hope of a better life.

<u>Land of Kaldalangra series</u>
(Suggested reading order)

The Lady of Steinbrekka

Heart of Kylassame

Soul of Asimina

<u>Stand-Alone Novels</u>

Finding Keepers

Alyssa's Bookshelf

Fragile Creatures - Kristina Circelli

The Helping Hands – Kristina Circelli

Beyond the Western Sun – Kristina Circelli

15 Minutes – Jill Cooper

Control You – Jennifer Snyder

Change of Possession – M.R. Polish

Natural Selection – Elizabeth Sharp

<u>Author Bio</u>

Fixing broken computers, wrangling a very spirited little toddler, and creating a world with a tyrant king, are all parts of the average day for Kristi Strong. While she has called Virginia her home for two decades, her head has rested in two countries, three states, and far too many houses to count. She was more than happy to give up her nomadic lifestyle and settle down with her husband, daughter, cat and chinchilla.

Connect with Kristi on
<u>Facebook</u>
<u>Twitter</u>
<u>Goodreads</u>
<u>Email</u>